A BUZZ FILLED THE ROOM ....

Def Cru 4 had arrived!

A scream of laughter came from the kitchen.

"Hi! Join the party!" Jennifer called out, moving toward the door.

The party was getting wilder by the moment. It went from noisy to a kind of frenzy. One of Def Cru 4's members said something to Kwame, and Kwame shook his head. The guy pushed Kwame away pretty hard.

There was a crash, and Sarah looked to see a lamp in pieces on the floor.

"Things are getting nasty," Dave said. "You want to split?"

"I don't know," Sarah said worriedly. "I don't want to leave Jennifer."

18 Pine St.

The Party

Written by
Stacie Johnson

Created by
WALTER DEAN MYERS

A Seth Godin Production

BANTAM BOOKS
NEW YORK • TORONTO • LONDON • SYDNEY • AUCKLAND

RL 5, age 10 and up

THE PARTY
A Bantam Book / September 1992

Special thanks to Judy Gitenstein, Betsy Gould, Amy Berkower, Fran Lebowitz,
Linda Lannon, Michael Cader, Pat Cummings, Helene Godin, and Lucy Wood.

18 Pine St. is a trademark of Seth Godin Productions, Inc.

ISBN 0-553-29720-1

Published simultaneously in the United States and Canada

Bantam Books are published by Bantam Books, a division of Bantam Doubleday
Dell Publishing Group, Inc. Its trademark, consisting of the words "Bantam
Books" and the portrayal of a rooster, is Registered in U.S. Patent and Trademark
Office and in other countries. Marca Registrada. Bantam Books, 1540 Broadway,
New York, New York 10036.

PRINTED IN THE UNITED STATES OF AMERICA

OPM 0 9 8 7 6 5 4 3 2

For Michael

18 Pine St.

There was a card shop at 8 Pine Street, and a shop that sold sewing supplies at 10 Pine that was only open in the afternoons and on Saturdays if it didn't rain. For some reason that no one seemed to know or care about, there was no 12, 14, or 16 Pine. The name of the pizzeria at 18 Pine Street had been Antonio's before Mr. and Mrs. Harris took it over. Mr. Harris had taken down Antonio's sign and just put up a sign announcing the address. By the time he got around to thinking of a name for the place, everybody was calling it 18 Pine.

The Crew at 18 Pine St.

Sarah Gordon is the heart and soul of the group. Sarah's pretty, with a great smile and a warm, caring attitude that makes her a terrific friend. Sarah's the reason that everyone shows up at 18 Pine St.

Tasha Gordon, tall, sexy, and smart, is Sarah's cousin. Since her parents died three years ago, Tasha has moved from relative to relative. Now she's living with Sarah and her family—maybe for good.

Cindy Phillips is Sarah's best friend. Cindy is petite, with dark, radiant skin and a cute nose. She wears her black hair in braids. Cindy's been Sarah's neighbor and friend since she moved from Jamaica when she was three.

Kwame Brown's only a sophomore, but that doesn't stop him from being part of the crew. Kwame's got a flattop haircut, dark glasses, and mischievous smile. As the smartest kid in the group, he's the one Jennifer turns to for help with her homework.

Jennifer Wilson is the poor little rich girl. Her parents are divorced, and all the charge cards and clothes in the world can't make up for it. Jennifer's tall and thin, with cocoa-colored skin and a body that's made for all those designer clothes she wears.

Dave Hunter is the boy next door. Sarah and Dave have been friends forever, but lately it seems like there might be something more. It doesn't hurt that Dave is a hunk—he's a basketball star, with a dazzling smile and a big heart.

April Winter has been to ten schools in the last ten years—and she hopes she's at Murphy to stay. Her energy, blond hair, and offbeat personality make her a standout at school.

And there's Billy Turner, José Melendez, and the rest of the gang. You'll meet them all in the halls of Murphy High and after school for a pizza at 18 Pine St.

PINE

One

"If it wasn't for pizza, extra everything, I simply could not cope." Jennifer Wilson pulled a chair up to the end of the table at 18 Pine St. Kwame Brown, Cindy Phillips, and the Gordon cousins, Sarah and Tasha, were already there.

"I got called on four times today in social studies and I only came up with three answers," Jennifer said. "And can you believe two of them were wrong?"

"The trouble is in the nature of history." Kwame, a short, stocky sophomore with black-framed glasses and mahogany skin, had finished his pizza and was scraping up the leftover cheese from his plate onto his index finger. "If all that stuff hadn't happened so long ago it would be a lot easier to remember."

"And nobody volunteered to help out," Jennifer went on. "Whatever happened to that sturdy crew of kids who just love to show off how smart they are?"

"Life is definitely hard, Jennifer." Tall, slender, dark-skinned Sarah was copying the math assignment from Kwame's small notebook. "But you have my sympathies."

"What are you doing after you finish your math homework?" Cindy asked. Cindy, pretty and petite, was Sarah's best friend. They'd known each other since Cindy's family had arrived from Jamaica when she was three. Sarah felt as if she could tell Cindy everything, and she often did, tying up the Gordons' phone for hours on end.

"I'm not sure. I'll call you." Sarah smiled at Cindy.

"And where is everybody today?" Jennifer said. "Here we are at the best pizza parlor in Madison, it's Monday afternoon, and the place is empty!"

"Probably recuperating from the party," Tasha said.

"Somebody gave a party and did not invite me?" Jennifer looked hurt.

"You didn't hear about the party over the weekend?" Sarah had finished copying the assignment

2

and was thumbing through the rest of Kwame's notebook. Her black turtleneck jersey set off her caramel complexion.

"The seniors gave a party to raise money for something," Tasha said. "I think they want to save the rain forests or something like that. They only raised thirty-three dollars but I don't think they really cared."

"Yeah, I heard it was something else." Kwame turned a chair around and straddled it.

"Anybody here go?" Jennifer asked.

"They only invited seniors," Kwame said.

"Who's Carol?" Sarah stopped at a name in Kwame's book.

"Yo, you can't go through my little black book," Kwame said, grinning as he grabbed his notebook.

"You keep your homework assignments in your little black book?" Sarah nudged Jennifer.

"How come I didn't hear about this party?" Jennifer asked.

"You remember when the school board was talking about giving the students a place to spend recreational time?" Sarah said.

"Go ahead." Jennifer took off her earrings, took out the opals set in them, and started replacing them with aquamarine stones.

"Girl, what are you doing?" Tasha asked.

"I thought today was an opal day," Jennifer said. "It's definitely not. Go on about the party."

"Letting the seniors hold a dance in the school gym was supposed to be the start of it," Sarah said.

"You ever see those old-time movies when everybody dances as long as they can," Kwame asked, "and the last person dancing wins a prize?"

"Yeah." Jennifer nodded. "Marathon dancing."

"Well, they called this party a Bop Till You Drop party," Kwame went on. "They had a computer set up and when you came in the door you got a number from the computer. Then every dance that came up, the computer matched you with somebody else and you had to dance every number."

"It had to be better than those stupid dances where all the boys sit on one side of the room trying to look cool and the girls end up dancing with each other," Cindy said.

"Where were you over the weekend?" Kwame asked Jennifer. "I called your house twice and you weren't home."

"Whoa." Tasha leaned back in her chair. "Check out Kwame. 'I called your house twice and you weren't home.' I didn't know you two were an item!"

"Kwame and I are definitely not an item!" Jennifer said. "Why were you calling my house, Mr. Brown?"

"You asked me to call," Kwame said, "remember? You said you wanted to go over the math."

"Oh, right," Jennifer said, remembering. "I was tied up."

4

"New guy?" Sarah asked.

"You've got a piece of cheese stuck to your chin," Cindy said, pointing at Sarah.

"I think it makes her look good," Tasha said. "Adds a certain flair. Maybe she'll start a trend. We can all wear a little food on our faces, maybe weave some spaghetti into our hair."

"Tasha, when you were in California you spent a lot of time in the sun, right?" Sarah asked. "And you didn't wear a hat?"

"Another Gordon fight?" Jennifer shook her head. "People are beginning to come to 18 Pine just to see if you two guys are going to get into an argument. It's better than a food fight."

Sarah was sorry that she and Tasha weren't getting along. She'd thought she had straightened everything out with her cousin, but lately the friction was back. Ever since her beautiful long-haired cousin had arrived to live in her house, Sarah's life had been turned upside down. She was sorry that Tasha's parents had died, but that didn't mean she had to let Tasha make her miserable. She decided to change the subject. "So what did you do this weekend, Jennifer?" she asked.

"It was Daddy's weekend," Jennifer said. "You know he gets one weekend a month in return for his weekly check. I got to sit in his outer office while he talked to some woman about having a stomach tuck."

"What is that, anyway?" Tasha asked.

"That's when they take the fat out from under the skin in your stomach," Jennifer said. "This woman was at least forty. She could have used a couple of tucks, a few lifts, and about a half pound of silicone for starters."

Jennifer Wilson's parents had been divorced recently. Sarah thought Jennifer was becoming an expert at persuading her father to finance her life-style as a way of easing his guilt. Between her mother and her father, Jennifer always seemed to be able to find a new skirt or blouse or piece of jewelry somewhere.

"Get to the good part," Sarah said. "What did he buy you?"

"We didn't even go shopping," Jennifer said.

"You didn't go shopping?" Tasha looked at Jennifer. "You have a father who's a plastic surgeon, making all that money, and feeling guilty about being divorced, and you did not go shopping?"

"The man had other things on his mind," Jennifer said. "He showed me beautiful downtown Providence for the umpteenth time, made another pitch for me to go to Brown, and indulged himself in our annual heart-to-heart chat."

"Sounds like you could use a good party." Tasha began to rock to a beat only she could hear. "I know I can definitely use a little noise and boys time."

"I've got to leave," Jennifer said. "My mom is

6

doing this big presentation in Washington tomorrow morning and I've got to help her get ready. I'll call you guys later. You going to be home, Tasha?"

"Where else?" Tasha asked. "We don't get time off for good behavior."

"Walk me down the street, Kwame." Jennifer had stood and was slipping on her jacket. "You can teach me all about adding exponents or whatever it was they were talking about in math today."

Kwame licked the pizza sauce off his fingers and stood as blond-haired April Winter came to the table.

"Is it something I said that makes you want to leave so quickly, Kwame?" April asked.

"It might have been," Kwame said.

"Good, write it down," April said. "I can use it next time, too."

"Do I get the feeling that I'm not loved?" Kwame asked.

"Here's a peace offering." April folded her slice of pizza and held it out toward him, pulling it back so he couldn't get too large a bite.

"I love your new haircut, April. Looks great. I'll talk to you later," Jennifer said as she and Kwame started toward the door.

"You know, I can't believe that Kwame can take that big a bite out of a piece of pizza without even opening his mouth wide," April said. She was delighted that Jennifer had noticed her new look.

"Tasha, you don't have to make our house sound

like a prison," Sarah said. "Because it's not, and I resent you saying things like that. You've only been living with us for a few weeks, and you make it sound like you hate it."

"Sarah, lighten up!" Tasha said.

"No, cousin, why don't you straighten up and check yourself out?" Sarah said. Tasha had been edgy for a while. She probably felt lost and alone, Sarah told herself, but the more Sarah tried to help, the worse it got. Sarah felt her face burn as she watched her cousin snatch her books up and move away from the table.

"What's eating her?" April asked.

"I don't know," Sarah said.

April started talking about the new uniforms the Murphy High basketball team had. Sarah's thoughts drifted back to Tasha. What had her mother said? That maybe Tasha felt uneasy about having to live with the Gordons.

"It's hard taking the fact that your parents have been killed," Mrs. Gordon had said. "And then to find yourself without a home, too. I'm sure it's not wonderful for her to have to live with her uncle. And people take loss in a lot of ways. We can't always expect them to act the way we think they should act."

"That girl never acts the way you think she should," Sarah complained to April.

"Sarah, you aren't even listening to what I'm saying." April shook her head.

"Oh, she just makes me so mad at times," Sarah said. "I really think she enjoys it, too."

"I can't figure you guys," April said. "I've known you since I moved here last year and you never argue with anybody except Tasha. I've known your cousin for a while now, and she never argues with anybody except you. You're pretty, she's pretty. You dress well, she dresses well. And when the two of you work together you're terrific. But you always fight!"

"That's her nature," Sarah said, gathering up her books.

"Hi!" Steve Adams, a recent transfer to Murphy High, stopped at the table just as Sarah was furiously stuffing her books into her backpack. He had been nice to Sarah ever since he had been unjustly accused of stealing a car. Sarah and her dad had helped Steve, and he was trying to show his gratitude.

"Sit down and talk to April, Steve," Sarah said. "I'm on my way home."

"You taking the bus home, Sarah?" April asked.

"No, I think I'll walk," Sarah replied.

Sarah left 18 Pine St. in a hurry. She had woken up in a good mood that morning. In fact, it was one of her best moods. She had even enjoyed the blue jay that squawked outside her window. She had taken a quick shower, put on her best blouse, the one that had just been demoted from party status to school status, had milk and a muffin, remembering to save a raisin muffin for the afternoon, and had even put the garbage out without waiting around for anyone to notice how wonderful she was. And, as usual, Tasha had spoiled the entire day with her nasty little comments.

Sometimes Sarah felt sorry for her cousin because Tasha had lost her parents in a car accident, but she sure wasn't any bargain to get along with. Still, there were days when Sarah liked her a lot, days when they seemed closer than she had imagined cousins could be.

By the time she reached the Gordon home on Evergreen, she had almost forgotten how angry she had been at Tasha. She reached the kitchen just in time to find her eleven-year-old sister, Allison, eating the last raisin muffin, the one that Sarah had so carefully saved for herself.

"Allison Gordon," Sarah said, "why are you eating my last muffin?"

"Oh, is it yours?" Allison asked.

"You know it was mine," Sarah said. "I announced it very loudly this morning just so nobody else would eat it."

"Are you suffering from PMS?"

"Don't you PMS me, you little snipe!" Sarah said.

"Joan of Arc died for her causes." Allison stood up. "I will die for a muffin. Be merciful and strike quickly!"

Sarah held the wooden spoon like a sword, pretended to lunge at her sister, and then threw the spoon on the table. They both laughed. Sarah opened the refrigerator, found half a container of strawberry yogurt, and took it out.

"That's Tasha's," Allison announced.

"Don't worry, I'll tell her you ate it," Sarah said.

"I only ate the first half," Allison said.

Sarah looked at the yogurt, then put it back in the refrigerator.

"Don't even think of eating the rest of it," she said, shooting what she meant to be a deadly glare at her sister.

Allison could be a pest at times, but Sarah couldn't think of a better eleven-year-old sister. Even when Tasha had first come to live with them and Allison had seemed to take Tasha's side in every argument, Sarah had never felt her sister had really abandoned her.

"Sarah," Allison asked, "you want to hear a great joke?"

"No," Sarah said.

"I'm bored," Allison complained.

"Go find someone your own size to pick on," Sarah said. She went into her room and closed the door. She took out her math book, turned to the page she had copied from Kwame's assignment book, and looked over the homework. Music. She couldn't face math without music. She switched the radio on and heard the hottest new reggae band. They were new to the charts but she liked their sound. Math could wait until after dinner.

"Sarah!" Allison's voice sounded far away. "Jennifer's here!"

"Go away!" Sarah said.

"Sarah!" Allison called again.

Sarah went out to the top of the stairs to call for Jennifer to come up, then decided to go downstairs instead.

"I've got a simply great idea for a party," Jennifer was saying.

Tasha was sitting with her chin on her hand at the far end of the kitchen table. Sarah decided not to mention their earlier argument.

"Hi, Tasha," she said. "Didn't know you were home."

"Is that why you scarfed down my yogurt?" Tasha said.

"I guess I shouldn't have mentioned I saw you with it," Allison said sweetly.

Sarah had to laugh. Tasha and Allison were made for each other. Even though they both frustrated her at times, she realized she was glad that both of them were part of her life. Once she and Tasha figured out a way to get along, everything would be fine.

"You guys want to fight or talk about our party?" Jennifer asked.

"Let's talk about our party," Allison said.

"Not your party," Jennifer said. "You're too young."

"Poo!" Allison gave a quick pout and went into the living room to watch television.

"Let's get a rap group to come to our party," Jennifer said. "I mean somebody kind of famous."

"I don't like rap," Sarah said.

"Sarah, rap is where it's A-T at," Jennifer said. "We're going to have a party that's going to put Murphy on the map. In fact, it's not going to be a party, it's going to be a par-tee."

"Why?" Sarah asked.

"If you have to ask why you need to have a party, then you won't understand the answer," Tasha said.

"Because we're not kids anymore," Jennifer said. "And we have to express that to the world. We have to say that we've moved to a different place, and a different time. We need to express stuff like that."

"I don't think I need to," Sarah said.

"I need it," Jennifer said. "I need to find myself, you know, get on with my life. What are we going to do, stay little girls until somebody gives us permission to move on?"

There was something in Jennifer's voice as she spoke. Sarah looked at her friend and saw that for once, Jennifer was serious.

"Hey, I'm with you, friend," she said. "I guess I could use a little noise and boys time, too."

PINE

Two

"So I asked her what she *thought* I would do with it?" Jennifer's voice sounded nasal when she was annoyed, and Sarah saw that she was very annoyed. The noise in the cafeteria did little to make her voice easier to listen to. "And she just came up with this old line about her knowing best because she's had experience. Well, how am I going to get experience with a credit card if she won't let me have one?"

"Jennifer, you already have a credit card," Sarah said. She picked at her food, then looked back up at Jennifer.

"But I can't get cash advances on it!" There was a

hard edge to Jennifer's voice. "She's going out of town this weekend and I have to live on whatever Mommy chooses to leave me. Suppose something happened?"

"Like what?" Sarah asked. Sarah knew that Jennifer was smart, and she was surprised at how easily her common sense was overruled when she got emotional. And she always seemed to get emotional when her parents were involved.

"Like anything!" Jennifer said.

The cafeteria at Murphy High was a huge, cavernous room with walls the color of watered-down pea soup and a cracked black-and-white tile floor dotted with many-colored stains that merely deepened with efforts to scrub them away. Because the school was so crowded, the cafeteria was open all the time, and students spent their free time studying and snacking.

At first the administrative staff tried to stop students from adding mustaches to the copies of Old Master paintings on the walls, but they eventually gave it up. The food was guaranteed to be nontoxic. Most of the students were happy when it was nonrecognizable.

Kwame walked into the cafeteria and headed toward them. He came up behind Jennifer and put his finger to his lips.

"Don't do it," Sarah said. "Jennifer's in one of her moods."

"I'm not in a mood and don't you dare do any-

16

thing!" Jennifer said, half turning in her seat. "Do you have to be so juvenile?" She stood, grabbed her books, and angrily brushed past Kwame.

"It's the rain," Kwame said. "Some people can't stand the rain. It depresses them."

"I don't know," Sarah said. "Something's bothering her. Yesterday she was anxious to talk about a party. Today she's just mad, mad, mad."

"She probably just needs a man's firm presence," Kwame said, nodding in approval of himself.

"You know anybody who would fit that bill?" Sarah asked, getting up from the table.

Kwame started to answer, watched as Sarah walked away from him, and then went back to work.

Sarah got to social studies as quickly as she could after math. Grabbing a seat next to Billy Turner's favorite one, she pulled out her notebook to study the list of debate topics.

"Hey, cuz, you still mad?" Tasha asked, slipping into the seat behind her. They had barely spoken to each other that morning.

"Hi, cuz." Sarah smiled and turned away. Tasha's timing for making up was the worst.

"I'm trying to be nice," Tasha said. She carefully balanced a stick of gum on Sarah's shoulder. "By the way," she added, "Allison confessed under torture so I let her finish the yogurt."

Sarah accepted the gum and switched her attention back to Billy, who was talking to Coach Green right outside the door. Only her complete concentration had kept his seat free so far but if Tasha kept yakking she might blow it. Billy Turner was the hottest star on the basketball team, and Sarah had decided that it might be interesting to get to know him better.

"So, what do you say, Sarah? Friends?" Tasha wouldn't keep still.

"Sure, of course," Sarah answered. Billy headed for the seat and somehow managed to swing his long legs up under the desk. He looked worried.

"I don't know what Coach told you to give up this time," Sarah teased, "but I'd be happy to give you a second opinion."

Billy turned to answer just as Mr. Cintron entered the classroom.

"All right, class. Come to order." The slightly balding teacher pushed his glasses up on his nose and started his daily walk around the outside perimeter of the desks.

"For the next few weeks we will be discussing the exchange of ideas in a democracy and the elements of effective debating…"

Mr. Cintron walked slowly past the windows, stopped in the corner, then walked along the back of the room, all the time explaining in great detail the differences between the pro and con sides in a debate.

"For and against," Tasha whispered sarcastically. "And I got it in under two seconds. Am I a genius or what?"

"What," Sarah said.

Tasha smiled and pushed Sarah's shoulder. Sarah was hoping they could go back to kidding each other, instead of just being mean. This seemed like progress.

"Tracy, please come up and record everyone's choice," Mr. Cintron called out. He had finished his introduction and handed a piece of chalk to Tracy, a quiet girl who had transferred to Murphy in mid-semester. Tracy had made few friends so far and having to stand in front of the class seemed to be too much for her. Her eyes stayed glued on the teacher.

"Okay," Mr. Cintron went on. "Four topics: six people each, three pro, three con. Let's start with 'Censorship in the Arts'... Who's against it?"

Half of the class raised their hands.

"Okay, Liz, Robert, Jill. Please make a note, Tracy. Now, who is pro censorship? Come on, this is the challenging part...Okay, Susan, Malik, Ayanna."

Sarah was waiting for "Steroid Use in Athletics." The moment the "ster..." left Mr. Cintron's mouth, her hand shot up. She didn't need to look at Billy. "Con" was definitely his position. The thought of the teamwork ahead made her grin. She knew at least a dozen girls who were nuts over this guy. And why not? He was delicious. She was already mentally scheduling a few one-on-ones with him to "discuss their topic."

"Okay, Tracy, that's Stefan, Alonzo, and Sarah," Mr. Cintron said.

Sarah managed a sideways glance at Billy not believing that he hadn't raised his hand to be on the con side. "Now pros?" Mr. Cintron asked. Billy still didn't raise his hand. Sarah slumped back in her chair, dazed. Bad enough that the long nights in the library were shot, but steroid abuse? Could it get more boring?

"And who wants the con position on 'Animal Testing for Medical Research'?" Mr. Cintron asked cheerfully.

Two hands went up.

"Sounds like a comment on our lunchroom," Tasha whispered in Sarah's ear.

Tracy listed the names as the muttering died down around the room. Sarah wondered if Billy had dozed off.

"Okay, that leaves 'Birth Control for Teenagers.' Who's left?" Mr. Cintron scanned the room.

Six people, Billy included, raised their hands. None of them seemed to care which side they took. Billy and Tasha ended up on pro against Tracy and two other students who were nearly as quiet as she was.

"Piece of cake," Tasha whispered in Sarah's ear.

Then she continued in a normal voice, "We gotta find Jennifer." The class was rustling papers, noisily copying names from the board. With the bell only a minute away, Mr. Cintron had taken off his glasses and was rubbing the bridge of his nose. That was the official sign to break camp.

"We need to get going on this party thing," Tasha went on. "Let's do this together, okay?"

Sarah swung around to face her just as the bell rang. When Tasha was nice like this, Sarah felt that they really were family, but right now she was only concerned with Billy's disappointing behavior.

"Sure, Tasha," she answered. Billy was already up and on his way out of the room. Sarah thought for a moment that he was ducking her but brushed the thought aside. "Jennifer's probably halfway through lunch already," she added.

"Mmmmm…I'm sure she's left us plenty of that delicious puppy chow, cousin dear," Tasha winked. "C'mon, I'm starving."

When Sarah and Tasha arrived in the cafeteria, they found April at their usual table. Dave Hunter was scarfing down something that looked like either a fried fish filet, an undercooked meat patty, or something that had gotten lost somewhere between the biology lab and the dumpster. Jennifer seemed somewhat calmer than she had earlier and was nodding wisely.

Sarah wasn't sure how she felt about seeing Dave. He had been her next-door neighbor and friend forever, but now things were changing. They had gone on a date, and there were definitely sparks flying. But now Dave seemed distant, as if he wasn't really interested. Sarah hadn't really thought about how her relationship with Dave's friend Billy might fit into all this.

"We need something big, something dramatic, something even the seniors didn't have," April said. "Something that people are going to talk about for a long time."

"What do you know about parties, April?" Cindy asked. She'd told Sarah that she didn't understand her letting this "kid" hang around her. April was sixteen, a year younger than Sarah and Cindy.

"No, she's right, Cindy," Jennifer cut in. "We do need something fresh. We need to out-party the seniors and let people know we can make our own decisions. I'm sick of them making decisions, always thinking that we have to just shut up and take whatever they dish out."

"What are you talking about?" Sarah had been quietly listening to Jennifer work herself into a sweat. "Who is this They and what are these Decisions? Nobody's said no yet, since we haven't even asked, right?"

"Get real, Sarah," Jennifer said. "You know the school's going to come down against a party if they even suspect that it's rocking."

"If they let the seniors have a party they'll let us have one," Dave said.

"Right," Jennifer said. "As long as it's something that's planned by children."

"What do you have in mind?" Sarah asked.

"I think I've got a hot idea," Jennifer said. She paused for greater effect and, leaning forward, looked around the table as if she were addressing partners in crime. "How about asking Def Cru 4 to perform?"

Def Cru 4 was the latest sensation in Madison. Combining rap with the Jamaican music, ska, they were a regular at local bars, and seemed poised to break through with a national record release. Sarah was a little uncomfortable with some of their lyrics, but she liked their rhythm. Cindy had told her that it must be the Jamaican influence—that's why they wore their hair in dreadlocks.

"Whoa," Tasha said. "I thought you were kidding last night. Why not just get impossible? How are we going to get up the money to get a group that's put out two albums already?"

"I heard they canceled the show in Westcove next weekend," Jennifer said. "Which means they're probably free."

"Right." Dave looked up. "And all we have to do is give them a call and they'll come running over to Murphy."

"With their dreadlocks," Sarah added.

"They'll never go for bringing them to Murphy," Dave said, shaking his head at the mere thought.

"It definitely won't hurt to try," Jennifer said. "If they don't charge too much, maybe I can get my dad to put up the money."

"Their lead singer is too much." Tasha closed her eyes as she talked. "He is long, lean, and lovely! I can just see us together in his—make that *our*—first video. I'll be in this slinky black dress and killer heels. Delight—that's his real name, too—will be all in black leather. I'll be looking mysterious and he'll chase me through the islands."

"How are you going to run in high heels?" April asked.

"Well, catching me is going to be the interesting part of the video."

The lunch crowd was breaking up just as Kwame came scooting over to the table with a tray piled high with desserts.

"Where's everyone going?" he asked. "Ahhh, Tasha. Sweets for the sweet." He offered her one of his desserts.

"Thank you, no," Tasha replied, looking offended. "My body is a temple that does not tolerate sweets."

"Yeah, the Temple of Doom," Sarah chimed in, then instantly wished she hadn't said it as the others around the table laughed.

"Cats can look at queens," Tasha said, standing

slowly. "And even make their little catty remarks."

Sarah looked at Tasha as she left the room and felt a stabbing pain in her chest. All her life she had worked to be nice, to be the girl everyone got along with. And now that her cousin had moved in—when it mattered so much that they get along—she couldn't figure out a way to turn her cousin into her friend.

PINE

Three

"Sarah, what are you doing?" Allison stopped in the kitchen doorway. Her best friend, Pamela Smith, was standing behind her with her chin on Allison's shoulder.

"What does it look like I'm doing?" Sarah asked.

"Messing up good food," Allison said.

"I'm preparing a special rice dish," Sarah said. "You don't have to eat it."

"Pamela and I want to use the table," Allison said.

"You need the whole table?"

"I guess not," Allison said. She settled down on one end of the table and put her notebook as close to

27

Sarah as she could, staking out her territory. "I've got our whole problem solved!" she announced to Pamela.

"You mean about the dolphins?" Pamela asked excitedly.

"Something even better." Allison was beaming. "We've already saved the whales, right?"

"Right!" Pamela agreed.

"Wait." Sarah looked up from the cookbook she was going through. "I thought people were still working on saving the whales."

"Well, we worked on that, too," Allison said. "Now it's time to move on."

"We have to use our time wisely," Pamela said.

"And we're effective," Allison added. "One week after we started working on freeing Nelson Mandela, he was free!"

"Wonderful," Sarah muttered to herself.

"What are we going to do now?" Pamela whined. She hated it when Allison joked around.

"Okay, okay." Allison wiggled her bottom in the chair, showing that now she meant business. "Okay, we were doing whales, right? Then the tuna thing, right? And you see what happened?" She paused but Pamela just stared at her.

"Everybody started doing them!" Allison was indignant.

"I thought we *wanted* everybody to help," Pamela protested.

"Yeah, but come on, Pammy, aren't you ready to do something else?"

"Okay, okay," Pamela said. "I'm tired of fishy stuff anyway."

"All right. First, swear you won't tell anyone until we're ready," Allison said.

"Okay, okay, I swear," Pamela said, raising her right hand. "Now, what is it?"

Allison looked around, satisfied that Sarah had left the room. "Gum control," she whispered.

"Gum control?" Pamela repeated. "I don't get it. You mean like maybe checking when you come into school to see if you're chewing gum or have some hidden in a book or something?" She was getting annoyed.

"No, silly. Look, what happens if somebody throws their gum in the river or something and it lasts for a thousand years and never breaks down?"

Pamela nodded.

"Okay, so what if a duck comes along and eats it, or maybe a dolphin, even!"

"Oh!" Pamela was shocked now.

"Then you're going to have ducks and dolphins going around filled up with old, chewed pieces of gum and choking and dying and everything! And suppose a whale ate it and it got stuck in his blowhole and he couldn't breathe and died!"

"It couldn't get stuck in his blowhole," Pamela said.

29

"Not even if it was bubble gum?" Allison asked knowingly.

The two friends looked at each other seriously and then shook hands. The new project had officially begun.

They were headed to Allison's room as Tasha and Mrs. Gordon came in the front door. Mrs. Gordon was carrying her briefcase and a bag of groceries and Tasha had a shopping bag.

"Allison, help set the table," Mrs. Gordon said.

"Okay, Mom." Allison shrugged at Pamela.

"Pamela, can you stay for dinner?" Mrs. Gordon asked.

"Nope, gotta go!" Pamela grabbed her notebook from the table and headed toward the door.

Dinner started calmly enough.

"Sarah, what's this in the rice?" her father asked.

"Pine nuts and sun-dried tomatoes. It gives the rice life!" Sarah said cheerfully. "Like it?"

"Very interesting," Mr. Gordon said. "Never hurts to try something different."

"Sarah really has a way with rice," Tasha said, smiling sweetly at her cousin.

"Allison, how was school?" Mrs. Gordon asked. "Did you find out about that field trip? You know, I might have to be in court next Wednesday."

"It's okay, Mommy." Allison was carefully pushing pine nuts and sun-dried tomatoes to one side of her plate. "Pammy's mom is coming. The aquarium only lets us come on Wednesdays, so it's gotta be then."

"What's happening with you two?" Mr. Gordon studied Sarah and Tasha.

"Jennifer's trying to get the juniors to have a party now, since the seniors had one," Tasha started. "A little relaxation."

"There was that Multicultural Festival in September," Sarah reminded her.

"Yeah, but that was the whole school. Besides, walking around the gym pretending you're in Spain ain't exactly a party," Tasha responded.

"Isn't," her uncle corrected her.

"Ain't, as in an expression, Uncle Donald—not ain't, as in bad grammar," Tasha said, to show that she knew the difference. Her uncle had been a teacher for so many years that he couldn't seem to stop talking like one.

Mr. Gordon's eyebrow raised a bit and he checked his wife's face to see if she thought Tasha was being fresh. But Mrs. Gordon was staring into the hallway in surprise.

"Good evening, all," Essie Gordon said as she sashayed into the dining room, bringing the scent of hibiscus flowers with her. She sat down and apologized for being late. "I had to take care of business," she said, winking at Sarah and Tasha. Those winks usually meant she was speaking their language as far as she was concerned.

31

Miss Essie, as everyone called her, had lived with the Gordons for almost as long as Sarah could remember. Sarah loved her grandmother. She smiled when Miss Essie walked in.

"And what business might that be, Mother?" Mr. Gordon asked, passing her the rice. She filled her plate and seemed very pleased with herself.

"And what business am I in, son?" she asked him. "What is the only business I have been in since you were in knee pants?" She was thoroughly enjoying this.

"Show business!" Allison sang out triumphantly. She didn't get what was going on but it was great to see Miss Essie so happy.

"Show business!" her grandmother confirmed. "This rice is magnifico. Bravo!"

Sarah couldn't help laughing. Miss Essie could be a bit theatrical on her good days. There hadn't been many of those in a while.

Mr. Gordon called her Mother, but no one else could call her anything but Miss Essie. Becoming a grandmother had been a shock to her when her career on Broadway was still based on parts as young singers or hatcheck girls. Later she had managed to get occasional television work, and even a continuing guest role on a series.

"What's going on, Miss Essie?" Mrs. Gordon asked, smiling cautiously. Her mother-in-law hadn't talked about her theatrical days in a long time. Nothing much had excited her, in fact, since her husband had died eight years ago. That had taken its toll on the whole family.

For a long while after her husband had died, Miss Essie could be found up in her room, staring out the window with Tarik Jones, her cat, asleep in her lap. She'd walk around the neighborhood a bit, sit out on the porch, maybe, or walk into a room so quietly that she'd make people jump. The last few years, she'd been gradually becoming more active. But tonight she was positively glowing.

"Jerry Swann called me again yesterday." She sounded almost girlish. "Me and him and Dad, we were all in a road show with the Douglas brothers...remember them?" Miss Essie saw that her son didn't have a clue who they were.

"Anyway," she went on, "he wants me for a commercial. He says I'm the 'perfect' person for the part."

"Hey, that sounds great, Mother," Mr. Gordon said. Jerry had offered her a part a while ago, but it hadn't developed into anything.

"Are you going to go for it, Miss Essie?" Tasha asked.

"You gotta do it, Miss Essie, it'll be fantastic. I'll be famous!" Allison was wondering if a TV-star grandmother could help with her gum control project.

"I'm thinking about it, honey," Miss Essie said softly.

"Whoa, that's wild," Tasha said, laughing. "Miss Essie on the magic tube."

"I don't see where it's funny, Tasha!" Sarah snapped.

"What is your problem, Sarah? Are you still mad because everyone liked Jennifer's idea?" Tasha shot back.

"Hey, this is still the dinner table, you two! What is going on?" Mr. Gordon was in it now. "What idea of Jennifer's?"

"That stupid party of hers," Sarah said. "She's just trying to prove something. She's on this kick about the juniors getting a party like the seniors..."

"The only thing you have against the party is that it wasn't your idea!" Tasha said icily.

"Look, you two," Mrs. Gordon broke in, "I don't know what you're arguing about, but I do think you can at least try to be civil to each other. You're both capable of rational discussion."

"If the juniors want a party and they are responsible about it, what is the problem, Sarah?" Her father turned toward her.

"I don't think we should get into this discussion," Mrs. Gordon said.

"I'm not getting into the discussion, dear," Mr. Gordon said. "I was just asking a question."

"That's getting into the discussion," Mrs. Gordon said.

"Jennifer's just tripping. She wants this rap group

to perform just to show up the seniors," Sarah said. "She thinks it's a big thing to get this group—Def Cru 4—so we can outdo the seniors. I don't think it's such a big deal." Actually, Sarah wasn't really sure why she didn't like the idea of the party. Something about it just didn't feel right. Maybe I'm scared, she told herself.

"Well, let it happen, then," her father said. "People have a right to be who they are."

"Dad!" Sarah felt worn out. Everybody seemed to be on Jennifer's side. She felt that Tasha was gloating.

"I just think you might be making too much of the whole thing," her father said.

"Can I be excused? I've got homework to do," she said quietly.

Her mother and father exchanged glances and then her father nodded.

"I'll do the dishes," Tasha said a little too eagerly.

That really made Sarah burn. She went up to her room feeling sick. The last thing she felt like doing was math.

PINE

Four

"I'm getting a case of terminal boredom, Sarah," Cindy complained, pulling her sweater closer around her shoulders. "They better wind this practice up soon or I'm out of here."

"Dave said they'd be through around sixish, Cindy," Sarah said. Being with Cindy always relaxed Sarah. Cindy was the one person in the world she could always count on.

"It's past six already." Cindy rearranged her books on the bench for the third time. They had been sitting in the stands watching the basketball team practice scoring on inbounding plays.

37

"I don't think Coach Green is, like, a warm-blooded mammal, you know?" Sarah hugged her jacket tighter. "I wish I hadn't told Billy I'd talk to him after practice."

"How can you and Billy spend all this time 'talking' when you and Dave are supposed to be the hottest item since Antony and Cleopatra?"

"That's why I need you here," Sarah said. "So it doesn't look like I'm trying to play up to Billy."

"But what about you and Dave?"

"I don't know. He just doesn't seem interested anymore," Sarah said. "I don't think it's me. I think he's worried about getting a college scholarship. He said his father's business was really off. Anyway, he's cooled down a lot."

"And Billy?" Cindy asked.

"I thought I'd give him a chance to impress me," Sarah said.

"You're going to get yourself in a lot of trouble playing games like that," Cindy said.

"I'm not playing games." Sarah laughed. "Just checking out the field a little."

"He knows about Dave, right?"

Dave didn't have the right to be jealous, Sarah thought. She had asked him out the first time they went on an official date. She had even coached him on what to say to her. What more did he want? She had liked him, maybe even loved him, but the only thing he was interested in was basketball. He lived, breathed, and ate basketball. She had hinted that he might take her out from time to time but he never seemed to get the hint. When he did finally ask her out it was to a college basketball game. He had spent the entire game rooting for one of the teams and punching her in the arm when they made a good play. Then, after the game was over and the team he was rooting for had lost, he sulked all the way home. Now he was jealous?

Billy, on the other hand, was a hunk. She liked him a lot, but if Dave was interested enough to be jealous, she didn't know what to do.

"We're supposed to be talking about social studies," Sarah said.

"Okay, so he's cool," Cindy said. "But is he impressing you?"

"He's working at it," Sarah said. "Look, it's breaking up."

"I hate sports," Cindy groaned. She stood and stretched, grabbed her things, and began picking her way down from the bleachers with Sarah.

"Lookin' good, brother," Sarah called to Dave as he and Billy approached.

"So, only Dave looks good, huh?" Billy asked with a half-smile.

"I won't kick you off the team," Sarah teased. "You definitely have potential. But right now we need to talk about social studies."

"Yeah, I guess so," Billy said. He glanced at Dave.

"Yo, man, if anybody can get you through social studies, it's Sarah," Dave said.

"Oh, Dave, you big star, can I carry your sweat-shirt?" Cindy asked in her girl groupie voice.

"Get out of here, Cindy," Dave said. "Look, Billy, I'll see you tomorrow. Don't study too hard."

Billy knelt and started taking off his sneakers as Dave and Cindy went off. Sarah thought about Cindy's kidding with Dave. When he answered her he had lowered his voice. That's what Dave always did when he wanted to act sexy. Sarah wondered if he was interested in Cindy.

"So, how you doing?" Billy asked when he had switched into his street sneakers. They were headed toward the same exit that Dave and Cindy had used.

"Okay, but you seem like something's bothering you," Sarah said. "Dave told me you were in danger of failing social studies and the coach was mad because you're not doing something or other—"

"Rebounding," Billy supplied the answer.

"Well, anyway, I know I can help with the social studies," Sarah said.

"Just got things on my mind," Billy said.

"Like, in Cintron's class, why didn't you go for that steroid business?" Sarah realized that Billy wasn't going to just start spilling his heart out. "You really seemed out of it. And look what you got stuck with, birth control for teenagers."

Billy stared straight ahead as if he was waiting for

words to appear on the wall. They went through the big double doors and into the side yard. He threw his sneakers onto a bench.

"I should have taken a shower," he said. "I probably stink."

Sarah sniffed twice. "You do," she said.

Billy smiled and sat on the back of the bench.

"Okay, look… This is private, okay?" He checked Sarah's face and, apparently satisfied with her nod, went on. "A buddy of mine is in some trouble. He's got this girl who wants to get married, you know. And he's not ready to get tied down."

"Is she pregnant?" Sarah asked.

"No, nothing like that," Billy said. "If he gets married, he'll probably drop out of school. That's the way those things usually go."

"Do I know this 'friend'?" she asked. She was sure it was Billy, but didn't want to push too hard.

Billy studied her again. "I don't know. You know a lot of people."

"Why doesn't he just break it off?"

"I guess you're right," Billy said. "I mean, he wants to do the right thing and all, but wow…"

"And you're upset because he's going to drop out of school?" Sarah asked.

"It's a lot of things," Billy said. "The girl's putting a lot of pressure on him. I hate to see a brother put in that position. You know what I mean?"

"I don't see why he has to drop out," Sarah said.

"I mean, it'll be easier if one of them finishes school, won't it?"

Sarah had worked part-time in a day-care center two summers before and several of the mothers who brought their kids there were barely older than she was. It had been rough for them. She had heard enough tales to know that she wasn't going to get caught in the early-marriage trap.

"The point is money, Sarah." Billy picked up a sneaker and played with the pump. "Not everybody has rich parents or a big house."

"Look," Sarah said pointedly, in case the "rich daddy" cut was aimed at her, "if it was me and some guy wanted to get married, or if I wanted to get married, I'd have to weigh everything and then live with what I decided. I'm sure your friend can do the same. People don't live in fairy tales anymore, and you can bet this guy's girlfriend isn't counting on some Prince Charming to rescue her."

"Yeah, I know that's right," Billy said. "And you can see it, but maybe she can't. Everybody's not like you."

"I don't know about that," Sarah said. "But you can't let it get you down."

Billy looked at her and smiled.

"You know," he said, "I liked it better when I was a stupid sophomore."

"You really looked good in practice today," Sarah said gently. "And I think your friend will be fine, really." She gathered up her books to go.

Billy reached over and ran his fingers down from her ear to up under her chin.

"Yeah, it'll be fine," he said. Then he kissed her softly with his hand still warm against her cheek. Sarah stopped breathing.

"Why, this corn is delicious!" Miss Essie was saying.

Sarah had no idea how she had managed the walk from the bus stop to her house. She felt liquid.

"Why, this corn is delicious!" her grandmother said again. The voice was coming from the living room, which struck Sarah as odd.

"Why, this corn is delicious!" Miss Essie exclaimed a third time. Sarah started to get a taste for corn, but the smells from the kitchen were decidedly meat-loafish. She found Miss Essie in the living room, standing in front of Tasha and Allison.

"One more time, Miss Essie," Allison insisted.

"And don't forget to flash those pearly teeth," Tasha said.

They all looked up as Sarah came in.

"Miss Essie's practicing her commercial." Allison was wearing one of her father's jackets.

"And what are you supposed to be, Allison?" Sarah grabbed her little sister and tickled her until she managed to wrestle free.

"I'm—I'm—" Allison was laughing and gasping

43

for air. "I'm the 'man-friend' who makes dinner for her, Sarah." Allison fell backward onto the couch.

"And all you made for her was corn?"

"I just cooked dinner..." she rolled onto her stomach, "...'cause we're on a..." she rolled smack onto the floor, "date!" She started giggling again.

"I'm going to convince Daddy to get you that lobotomy, little girl," Sarah teased. The jacket had opened and Sarah saw a round piece of pink construction paper taped to Allison's shirt.

"All they're advertising is this margarine spread, so that's all I'm supposed to go on about." Miss Essie had settled back in an armchair and was studying a stack of papers.

"What's this?" Sarah asked, tapping the pink paper. It looked like some sort of political button. All Sarah saw was the word "Control." She figured it was another one of her sister's secret projects designed to save the world.

"Eeeeeeeeeeeeeeeek," Allison screeched and ran from the room.

"I hate when she does that," Tasha groaned.

"You girls cut it out," Miss Essie chided, not even looking up from her papers. "I'm studying my lines. Leave that baby alone."

Sarah and Tasha exchanged looks. They weren't exactly kissing cousins after the other night's argument, but they did see eye to eye on one thing: Allison was no baby. Or angel. Or cupcake. Or sweetie pie. Or any of the things Miss Essie called her.

"It's one of her projects," Tasha explained. "Don't ask."

"Sarah," Mrs. Gordon called from the kitchen, "April's on the phone."

Sarah ran up to her room, grabbed the phone, and slid onto the floor.

"What's up?" Sarah wanted to tell someone about what Billy had said, but April wasn't the one. It had to be Cindy.

"You know the Def Cru 4 concert? Are you, like, going?" April asked. "Because I don't get it, I swear…It's not like I don't get it—I mean I get it. I'm sure it's like an art form, but is it music or what?"

"Think of it as poetry, April," Sarah advised. They had had this discussion before. "Explaining Rap 101," Sarah liked to call it.

"I know, I know, Sarah…but are you going? I mean, I can understand yodeling if I think about it, but that kind of makes sense, you know? Like, say you're stuck on a mountain top or trapped in an avalanche or something so you need to start yelling to get some attention, and all, but, this is talking, not really music, is it?" She paused for breath and Sarah jumped in quickly.

"I don't think I'm going, April. Maybe Tasha and Jennifer are, but I'm not into it enough to shell out twelve bucks." Sarah heard a curious thump in

45

Allison's room. "But listen," she said, wanting to wind this conversation up, "I think you ought to go. It would help you understand what the attraction is."

"By myself?" April whined.

"Call up that guy with the cute butt. What's his name. George Davis. Maybe he'll go with you."

"I wish."

"Well, you'll bump into people you know, anyway," Sarah said.

"Okay. Okay. I'm going to do this. It'll be like research...sort of educational, you know. I can handle this." April was pumping herself up, talking herself into facing an uncomfortable situation. That was something about her that Sarah admired. April's childhood of moving from place to place because of her father's troubleshooting job with a huge computer company had made her very quick on her feet. Even when a situation made her nervous, Sarah had seen April dive into it and start swimming for all she was worth. The only thing was that she needed a revving-up session first.

There it was again. A soft thumping. Like a softball rolling off a bed.

"I gotta go, April." Sarah wanted to be supportive. "Do it."

"Okay," April said. "I'll be there."

"Good," Sarah said.

She hung up and thought about April. Sometimes she babbled a bit too much, but the girl was really game. Underwater exploration. First woman on the moon. Open-heart surgery in a telephone booth. She would do it.

Thump.

Sarah went and knocked on Allison's closed door. It was plastered with signs that read "Stay Out" and "Do Not Enter, Or Else" and one sign Sarah had never figured out that had bright red and black scribbles above the words "guts and eyeballs."

"Allison, you okay?" It got very quiet inside. "It's time for dinner, kid, you going to set the table?"

"I'm coming," Allison called out. "Don't come in."

Tasha came up the stairs and saw Sarah standing outside of Allison's door.

"What is going on in there?" Sarah whispered.

"I don't know," Tasha said. "But I'm not going in. She's probably found a way to turn intruders into goats or something."

"Or little heaps of 'guts and eyeballs.' We'd better be careful," Sarah said, pointing to the sign.

"Let's get Uncle Donald to talk to her," Tasha said. "Fathers love to talk to little girls."

Tasha held up her hand and Sarah gave her five. Sarah felt terrific. This was what it was like to have a cousin for a friend. She'd have to remember to thank her sister. Sarah wondered what kind of secrets Allison could have.

PINE

Five

If Jennifer had asked her to go shopping in person, Sarah would have given her a friendly but firm no. But when Tasha had delivered Jennifer's message in the hallway at Murphy High, and had stood there looking at her just knowing she would say no, Sarah decided to go.

"You're going?" Tasha had looked shocked.

"It might be fun," Sarah had said.

Now that she was waiting for Jennifer in the Westcove Mall she knew she didn't want to be there. She certainly didn't feel like watching Jennifer demonstrate how much money she could spend on clothes she didn't need.

"Oh, Sarah! How are you?" Sarah turned to see Jennifer and her mother. Jennifer's mother, an interior decorator with her own business, looked great as usual. She was wearing a sharp blue suit with a green scarf and an amber pin on the lapel.

"Hello, Mrs. Wilson," Sarah smiled.

"Mom's finally going to buy a new overnight case," Jennifer said. "She was on her way to the mall, so I hitched a ride. You should see the thing she's been using."

"It's serviceable," Mrs. Wilson said. "But I can use a new one. I'll leave you girls on your own. See you at home, Jennifer. And don't be too late."

"Yes, Mother." Jennifer let her eyes roll up.

"And what are we looking for today?" Sarah asked when Jennifer's mother had started toward the department store at the far end of the mall.

"I can use a new sweater," Jennifer said, taking Sarah's arm. "Did Tasha tell you what happened in school today?"

"No, we aren't exactly seeing eye to eye these days," Sarah said.

"Well, I went to the office to ask about the party. I was going to do it the right way. Say 'pretty please,' the whole thing. Okay?" Jennifer looked furious. "I talked to that creep Schlesinger. How did he ever get a job like assistant principal?"

"What happened?" Sarah asked. Jennifer rarely

50

had any worries that a little something from the mall couldn't fix.

"Mr. Schlesinger starts telling me that I have to go to the student council when they meet again and get their approval to request permission to have a party. I don't even know when they meet." Jennifer nudged Sarah as a heavyset boy broke away from a group of other boys and swaggered toward them. "I wonder what this fool wants!"

"Yo, Mama, I just had to come over here and tell you how sweet you look," the boy said, glancing back to make sure his friends were watching him.

"Don't call me your Mama," Jennifer said. "Because if I was your Mama I would have killed you when you were a child so I wouldn't have to put up with you today."

"I was only trying to pay you a compliment!" the boy said. "That's what's wrong with sisters today. Too stuck on yourselves."

The boy made a gesture of dismissal toward the girls and swaggered back to his friends.

"That was kind of harsh, Jennifer," Sarah said.

"I know," Jennifer said. "But I'm in no mood to deal with fools. Anyway, so then Mr. Schlesinger tells me that it doesn't matter anyway because there's already an event planned for the juniors. I don't remember voting on an event, do you?"

"What event?" Sarah asked, hoping Jennifer would calm down if she talked to her quietly.

51

"Oh, that's the best part." Jennifer was just gathering steam. "Are you ready for this? A bowlathon. Get that? And you know nobody that we know voted for a stupid bowlathon!"

"Wait a minute," Sarah said. "Didn't we vote for a bowlathon around the second day of school? Remember someone was talking about us doing a Feed the Homeless Walk?"

"Oh, that's what he's talking about?" Jennifer stopped in front of a window featuring jeans and leather jackets. "Maybe, but that's not like a party activity."

"We did vote for it, though," Sarah said. She wondered why Jennifer had wanted to talk to her.

"Anyway, I was thinking," Jennifer said. "We just have to have the party at my house."

"Your mother doesn't even like us coming over and hanging out," Sarah said. "She'll have a fit!"

"She's always going away on decorating jobs," Jennifer said. "I'd need help in cleaning up afterwards, but we can pull it off. She'll never even know we had one."

"I don't know," Sarah said. "Anyway, if you had a lot of kids over it could be a mess. It could cost a lot, too."

"My dad will spring for the bucks," Jennifer said. "I called him this morning. Of course, I didn't mention that Mom was going to be out of town. But then again, he didn't ask me, either. Anyway, he went for it. He wants me to like Shawnee, so he'll do anything."

"Shawnee?" Sarah looked at Jennifer. "What is Shawnee?"

"Oh, didn't I tell you about Shawnee?" The corners of Jennifer's mouth tightened. "I told you I went up to Providence to see him, right?"

"Yeah."

"So when I get there I see this woman. She's about twenty-five, right?"

"Twenty-five? As in twenty-five years old?" Sarah stopped and turned toward Jennifer. "How old is your father?"

"He's forty-four. Old enough to be Shawnee's father," Jennifer said.

"Shawnee? Is she black?"

Jennifer nodded. "All she does is grin and talk about her tennis game. If you can imagine a brown Barbie doll with a blond wig and little brown eyes that open really, really wide because she is always so, so surprised at Life with a capital L, then you have this babe down to a T."

"You trying to say you don't like this woman?" Sarah asked.

"No, she's okay," Jennifer said. "I just wasn't in the mood for her this weekend. Let's look in the pet store."

"You're going to buy a pet?"

"No, just looking." Jennifer pulled Sarah into the pet shop.

"I still don't know about having a party when your mother's away," Sarah said.

"Oh, come on, Sarah!" Jennifer said. "I mean, I really need your support. I never ask you for much, right? But you can help me get the house ready and stuff like that. You're good at planning things, too. Okay?"

"I guess so," Sarah heard herself saying. "Look at that puppy. He's a dalmatian."

"I can't buy a dalmatian," Jennifer said. "The only clothes they go with are basic black."

"Jennifer!"

The two girls looked at the other puppies, talked to the huge parrot, and left the pet store.

"Here comes my mom," Jennifer said. "Watch what you say."

Sarah felt uncomfortable as Mrs. Wilson approached them. She was carrying a small package.

"Did you find a bag, Mrs. Wilson?" Sarah asked.

"No, so I consoled myself with some perfume." Mrs. Wilson held up her package. "Shalimar. I used to use it all the time but then I decided it was a little heavy."

"It is," Jennifer said.

"Well, I'm going to try it again," Mrs. Wilson said.

"Oh, Mom, is it okay if I go to a concert with Tasha this Thursday?" Jennifer asked her mother. "It's going to be in Willowdale."

"What kind of concert?" her mother asked, taking out her car keys. "Are you going home now?"

"Sarah and I are still shopping," Jennifer said. "And the concert is this rap group I like."

"How would you get there?" her mother asked.

"Mom, believe me, I'll find a way," Jennifer said. "Look, going to Willowdale is no big thing!"

"I don't know, honey," her mother answered. "Your math grade makes me think that you need to put in a little more time studying and less time hanging out."

"Hanging out?" Jennifer's hands went to her hips. "Hanging out?"

"Yes, hanging out, young lady. You might do better if you cut back on all that time you spend at the mall, too." Mrs. Wilson had a habit of turning her head slightly to one side when she was annoyed, and she was definitely annoyed with her daughter. "I've been meaning to talk with you about how you budget your time."

"Budget my time?" Jennifer's voice rose. "You mean how you want to budget my time, right? Well I don't need you to plan my time, thank you."

"Watch your tone, miss, or you won't have to worry about your free time at all," her mother said firmly. "If you want to be treated like an adult, then you're going to have to start taking some responsibility, Jennifer."

"Oh, great. You won't let me take responsibility

for a cash card but everything else is on me, right?"

"If you can't take responsibility for your math, if you can't do better than a C-minus, then no. No, you aren't ready for a cash card."

"What am I going to do with stupid math?" Jennifer was escalating the argument. "Go around the rest of my life looking for triangles to measure?"

"Perhaps you can use it to go to a good college," her mother said. "As I did."

"Oh, like you need a Ph.D. to pick just the right throw pillow to go with the wallpaper?" Jennifer snapped. Her expression showed that she was sorry about her remark the moment it left her mouth.

"Jennifer, this conversation is over!"

"Can I go to the concert or not?" Jennifer persisted.

"No!" Jennifer's mother turned and walked quickly away.

Sarah watched Mrs. Wilson until she reached the down escalator, then turned to Jennifer. She had known Jennifer for most of her life but had never seen her like this. Mrs. Wilson must really be hurting, Sarah thought. After the breakup of her parents' marriage, Jennifer had become even more demanding.

"You ought to put either your temper or your mouth on hold," Sarah said.

"She doesn't want me to do anything," Jennifer said. "I'm stifled! You know how that feels?"

"Why do you need a cash card?" Sarah asked.

"I don't need a cash card," Jennifer said. "That's just the point. She gives me what I need because that's her job. You're a mother, you have a job. The job is to give the kid what it needs. But I want her to have a relationship with me. Give me something I don't need, that's what relationships are about."

"I'll have to think about that one," Sarah said.

Jennifer was crying. The tears ran down her face as she moved away from Sarah. Sarah looked at her friend's image in the plate-glass window of the pet store. She hated to see a fight between any of her friends and their parents. Nobody ever seemed to win those fights. It reminded her of her fights with Tasha.

The two girls walked through the large, nearly empty mall together for a while without speaking. Sarah thought about how it would be to own one of the stores and decided that she wouldn't want to. What she didn't think about, what she refused to think about, was the party. She didn't want to be part of doing something behind Mrs. Wilson's back, but she had just promised to do exactly that.

Six

"Ladies, ladies, ladies! I have arrived," Kwame crooned as he swung into a chair at 18 Pine St. next to Sarah and Jennifer. Sarah was having French fries and a soda and Jennifer had a mini-pizza with mozzarella and walnuts. Tasha was drinking milk and eating raisins from a bag she had brought with her. The three girls ignored Kwame.

"I gotta do it, Tasha," Jennifer was saying. "What's the worst that can happen? I'm missing the concert already."

"Hold it, did somebody say 'Def Cru 4'?" Kwame asked. "And would any of you lovely ladies be attending this fine cultural event unaccompanied and in need of a man's protection?"

"Are you paying for us, Kwame?" Tasha asked.

"Paying? Oh."

"*Oh?*" Tasha looked at Jennifer. "Did he just hit us with a very lame 'Oh'?"

"That he did," Jennifer said.

"I think I have to go," Kwame said.

"I hope mere money is not going to come between us?" Jennifer called after Kwame as he beat a hasty retreat.

"I think money has definitely come between you and Kwame," Tasha said. "That guy never has any money."

"And, speaking of Def Cru 4, guess what semifamous sophomore called me last night to inform me that she is going to the concert," Sarah said. "Her initials are April Winter."

"You have got to be kidding me," Jennifer cut in. "April is going and I'm on house arrest?" She shook her head.

"It's a free country, Jennifer," Sarah responded. "And it's certainly not April's fault that you aren't going."

"I didn't say it was," Jennifer said.

"You talk as if you own these guys," Sarah said. "I mean, do you actually know them? Like in 'Yes, I have met them and talked to them in person'?"

"No, but I know people who know them," Jennifer protested. "And who put you in charge of the world today?"

"Well, why do you keep going on like you're supposed to be the only one who goes to see them?" Sarah asked.

Jennifer didn't answer. "I'll see you later, Tasha," she said pointedly. She got up and left their table and went and sat with Steve Adams and his friend.

"What's with her, anyway?" Sarah said after Jennifer had left.

"She's having one more try at having the party in the school," Tasha said. "So you ought to like that, at least."

"What's eating you?" Sarah asked.

"Oh, just the usual, cuz," Tasha answered. "Nothing a little party wouldn't fix…you remember, party? Like the one we were going to work on together with Jennifer?"

"You really think the idea is that great?" If their friends were sick of their fighting, Sarah was even sicker.

"Look, there comes a time in your life when you need a party. Everybody wants a party. If you don't want to be part of the solution, fine," Tasha said. "But do you have to be part of the problem?"

"No, I don't," Sarah said. "Look, can we have a truce on this?"

"Just call me Lucy because I love a little trucey," Tasha agreed. She reached into her bag and pulled out a stick of gum and offered it to her cousin. Sarah took it and wondered how long the truce would last.

Afternoons in Murphy High were best for Sarah when she was in Mrs. Bender's English class. The woman could make English seem like a positively wonderful course.

"Did you finish the third act yet?" Cindy asked over her shoulder.

"I read it, but don't ask me about it," Jennifer answered. "It's another language."

"Okay," Mrs. Bender began. Beatrice Bender had been named after Beatrix Potter, who wrote the Peter Rabbit stories. She had made the mistake of telling the class about her namesake. There was no going back. "Cottontail" and "Flopsy's Mama" were two of the nicer nicknames she had been given. In fact, she looked a little rabbit-like because of an overbite and a turned-up nose. But she was an excellent teacher and well liked.

"Okay," she repeated. "Act three, scene two...Jennifer, you're Hamlet."

Jennifer groaned. This stuff was hard to read and impossible to recite. She made a great deal of commotion opening her book, adjusting her posture, clearing her throat.

"Jennifer?" Mrs. Bender was growing impatient. "From 'Speak the speech,'"

"'Speak the speech, I pray you,'" Jennifer began.

"'As I...as I pronounced it to you...' What is this 'trippingly'? 'Trippingly on the tongue'?" Jennifer looked up from the book and instantly lost her place. There were a few snickers.

"Trippingly. Smoothly," Mrs. Bender said. "He is asking the actors to say his words the way that he has told them to say them. He wants to be sure they don't flub their lines. Delivery is important to him. Did you all get that, class?"

There were a few groans of assent.

"When you read poetry to yourself, it's one thing," Mrs. Bender said. Reading Shakespeare after lunch was asking for trouble. "Speaking it aloud is something else. It has to flow, like music, like..."

"Like rap," said Jennifer. She thought Delight was a poet with a capital P. That brother could spin some words trippingly.

"Well, yes, I suppose. Like rap." Mrs. Bender noticed all eyes were open, waiting to see where she was headed. "If you look at the lyrics to some rap, er...ah, tunes, you will probably find that the rhythm is important. How the rhyme is said is almost as important as what is being said. For example, give me a lyric to a rap song, someone."

Across the room someone must have muttered something juicy, because the rows by the door burst into laughter.

"Something repeatable, please," Mrs. Bender chided.

"Who's to blame, is it the people or the President? Our people are oppressed by the leaders of our government," offered Dave. A couple of people did sound effects in the background.

"Okay, class. The point is that the delivery matters almost as much as the message, right?" Mrs. Bender eyed the class. "Who did that poem, Dave?"

"Def Cru 4." Dave was grinning.

"Well, very nice, very nice." Mrs. Bender cleared her throat and returned to working through Hamlet line by line. At the end of class she surprised them all.

"Okay, review act three for Monday and jot down any questions. Also," she added with a little glint in her eye, "bring some more rap lyrics, if you will. Please write them out, and we'll take a look at some, shall we say, more modern poetry, all right?"

Rap? In English? Sarah thought Monday would be interesting.

Seven

"*Jennifer's on the phone!*" Allison shouted at the top of her lungs.

"Where did they find you, you heathen?" Tasha demanded and snatched the phone from Allison's hand. "Yeccchhh, what is this? The phone's all sticky…Hi, Jennifer?"

"Mommmmm, Tasha's teasing me again," Allison howled and went toward the kitchen looking for support.

"No, it's just Allison, the human siren…so what are you saying? Slow down," Tasha said. Jennifer was speaking too fast to make sense. "What? Sure, fine, come on over." Tasha hung up the phone as Sarah was signaling for her to tell her what was up.

"What was all that about?" Sarah asked.

"Allison's brain was rattling around her head again," Tasha said.

"No, I mean on the phone," Sarah said.

"That was Jennifer. She's on her way over with some, as she put it, 'unbelievable news.'" Tasha looked skeptical.

"It's either got to do with the party or she heard she was passing math," Sarah said, then quickly added, "I know, I know, I said I'd help out and I will. I just feel a little like this unbelievable news will be something totally believable?—for Jennifer. Nothing that girl does will surprise me." Sarah collapsed onto the couch. Saturday was her stay-at-home day, and it was off to a great start.

"About a year ago she got into an argument with the owner of a manicure salon. Over a manicure! Jennifer wanted a silk wrap and the woman didn't want to do it and Jennifer wouldn't leave the shop. They actually called the police. What a mess!"

"Sounds good to me," Tasha said. "She was sticking up for her rights."

Allison came into the room with Mrs. Gordon, stopped in the middle of the floor, and pointed toward Sarah and Tasha.

"There they are!" she announced. "They are the ones who unjustly attacked me!"

"Girls, I'm going to the office for a few hours," Mrs. Gordon said. "If either of you happens to kill Allison before I get back *please* don't leave her body in the middle of the floor."

"Mom!" Allison tried to fake a hurt look, gave it up, and made a dash for the stairs before Tasha or Sarah could grab her.

Mrs. Gordon was about to leave when the phone rang. She stayed to see if it was for her. It was April. "I don't see why I even think it could be for me," Mrs. Gordon said. "See you later."

Sarah spoke briefly to April and hung up. "She's on her way over," she said.

When the doorbell rang and Pamela showed up, Tasha wondered aloud if the Gordon household was getting to be a shelter for the homeless. Pamela didn't seem to mind the remark as she clumped noisily up to Allison's room.

"Those kids are getting weirder and weirder," Tasha said and sank into an armchair. "We should go up there, break their door down, and reveal their evil doings to the world."

"I was never that weird," Sarah said.

"We'd get shot if we went up there," Tasha said.

Sarah paused to consider Tasha's warning and settled down on the couch with her. "Slimed, maybe. De-gutted or de-eyeballed, perhaps," she said thoughtfully. "But I really don't think they're armed. Mom would have mentioned it."

The doorbell rang again, and Sarah opened the door.

"Yo, yo, yo, yo…April Winter is in the house," April said as she went by into the living room. She wore a baseball cap pulled down backward over a mass of blond braids.

"Oh, no." Tasha moaned. "This isn't happening. April, tell me those aren't dreads you're going for, please."

"I'm a babe from the block and I didn't come to shock, sh-sh-sh-shock you…" April bobbed her head in imitation of a rapper.

"Uh, April." Sarah went back to her seat on the couch. "Have a seat, homegirl, I think the sun has done you in."

"C'mon, guys, it's me. April. I'm a 'round-the-way girl, you know? I'm down." April removed her cap to reveal the tangle of hastily braided hair. April giggled, and the three of them started laughing. They ended up on the floor.

"You did that yourself, did you?" Tasha asked between gulps of air.

"Who else?" April slipped out of her jacket.

"So what was the concert like?" Sarah asked.

"Wild. Absolutely wild," April said.

"You go by yourself?"

"No," April looked down at the floor. "I called Steve Adams and asked him if he was going and he said he wasn't but that he might. And so he did."

"You did what!" Tasha got up on her knees just as the doorbell rang. "You went on a date with Steve Adams and failed to get my permission? What are these children coming to?"

Jennifer was at the door and by the time Sarah brought her into the living room she had been told that April had been at the concert.

"More about Steve later," Tasha said. "Tell us about the concert."

"Okay." April began again. "So like they came out and they had this, like, smoke effect and these girls were on the stage dancing." She took a breath.

"And, then this guy Delight comes out. Unbelievable. You should have heard him. He used all those words you get suspended for using in school," she said. "And he used them over and over again. And those girls were doing some wild dancing. If they ever did that act in Murphy High the paint would come off the walls. I mean, this isn't like the stuff we listen to on the radio."

"April, you just wasted a ticket, you know?" Jennifer was obviously annoyed. "Delight is a poet. And you have to look beyond the language to understand his message."

"Excuse me, Miss Rocket Scientist," April shot back. She reached into her jeans pocket and produced a small pad that was scribbled over with purple ink. "I may not be on your level, Jennifer, but I think I can understand a message that I've seen scribbled on walls with little dirty drawings," April said. "And if I didn't understand what he was saying, he had all those dancers doing pantomime!"

April plopped down on the couch. Sarah began clapping. "Bravo, Bravo!" she cheered. "Two points for April's team."

"Cut it, Sarah," Tasha said, narrowing her eyes at her cousin. "We're all on the same team, right?" Sarah got the message. She didn't want to break their truce.

"What's your incredible news, anyway, Jennifer?" Tasha asked.

"Okay, I've made the final decision." Jennifer gave April a withering gaze. "I'm having the party at my house." She paused. No one said a word.

"My dad'll help with money for food, and anything else we need to buy. And people can bring things. You guys will, right?"

Tasha nodded and Sarah joined in reluctantly.

"It can be next weekend. It's practically together because..." and Jennifer paused dramatically.

"Because? Because?" Tasha prompted her. Jennifer could be so theatrical.

"Because, I got Def Cru 4 to come!" Jennifer was ready to pop. "Could you just die?"

"No, Jennifer, I could not just die." Sarah shook her head.

"Wait a minute," April was interested now. "You weren't even at the concert. How did you manage to get them to come?"

"Simple," Jennifer said. "I have a friend who knows their lighting guy. She gave me the name of their hotel. I just called them and invited them to the party. They said they would love to come to a party. Delight said they wouldn't do a whole show at the party but they would come and they would probably do at least one number."

"You spoke to Delight?" Tasha asked.

"Sure," Jennifer said.

"That's, like, totally awesome," Sarah said, doing her best Valley Girl impression.

"Isn't it wild?" Jennifer agreed. She didn't seem to realize Sarah was making fun of her.

"So what can we do to help?" Tasha asked quickly before Sarah got wound up. "Did your mom set a limit on how many people you can invite?"

"Well…" Jennifer hesitated. "My mom won't exactly be there."

"I don't blame her," Tasha said. "It might get a bit loud with Def Cru 4 there. Is she warning the neighbors before she heads for the hills?"

"Tasha, I haven't told her about this yet," Jennifer said sheepishly. "I don't think it would be a big deal."

"I'd like to see her face if she comes in and sees some of those dancers," April said.

"It's just that she's got this big job she's working on." Jennifer rushed on. "It's, like, really important to her career and all and I didn't want to bother her with all of this right now."

"Does your dad know about the party?" Sarah asked. She knew Jennifer hadn't told him, but wanted to let Jennifer tell the others.

"Not exactly," Jennifer said.

"Let me get this straight," Tasha said. "You're going to turn over the house to a bunch of rappers you don't even know and your mother and father don't know about it?"

"Tasha, I'm seventeen years old," Jennifer said. "Eventually I have to live my own life. I can't be my mother's child for my entire life. And my father gave up his right to tell me what to do when he split!"

"And Tasha, you think this is a really cool idea, right?" Sarah turned to her cousin.

"Sarah, enough. You do what you want to do," Tasha said evenly, "but don't give me advice. We said we'd help, and that's what I'm going to do. I don't have all these conditions and rules attached to my word when I give it. I just do it."

"Sarah, what you pass off as okay is any rules that anybody in the world shows you. If you see rules you follow them, simple as that." Jennifer was near tears. "Did it ever occur to you that sometimes the rules just don't work?"

The room was quiet except for the soft sound of Jennifer's sobbing. Sarah could hear a television set somewhere and thought it was probably coming from the den.

"I guess I'll just be running along now," April said weakly. "I think I'll just show myself out. Yesireee."

"Well, Jennifer," Tasha started pleasantly, ignoring Sarah standing there with her hands on her hips. "I guess that leaves just you and me."

"I guess so!" Sarah turned and ran up the stairs.

In her room, Sarah sat curled up on her bed. Maybe she was being a goody-goody, and maybe the rules were important to her. They had always worked for her before, she thought, and now she wondered why they suddenly seemed so restrictive. With Tasha things seemed so simple. Things just weren't that simple for Sarah.

PINE

Eight

What Sarah felt, more than anything, was alone. Her
gut feeling said that Jennifer's party was wrong.
Sarah didn't like sneaking around doing anything.
Still, she hated the idea of going against everybody.
She went to the bathroom and looked at herself. Her
hair was a mess and her face looked hard with ten-
sion.

She took deep breaths, trying to calm herself
down, trying to bring herself to a point at which she
could make a decision.

"So what are you going to do, kid?" she asked
herself.

She remembered what her father had told her years before. When you have a hard decision to make, the first thing you had to decide is who you are. Was she the kind of person to sneak around to a party? Or was she a person too bound by rules to have fun? When she'd been younger she'd never had any problems deciding who she was.

Maybe, she thought, that was the reason she was having problems now. She wasn't younger anymore. Now she had to start making decisions as a young woman, not as a kid. Sometimes, everything wasn't so cut and dried.

Sarah walked out of the bathroom with her head high. She started down the stairs and saw Jennifer standing at the door, just ready to leave.

Jennifer looked up at her. They had been friends for so many years. Sarah forced a smile as she came to the foot of the stairs.

"I'll bring a salad," she said. "And I'll help anyway I can."

"Thanks, Sarah." Jennifer came over and touched the back of Sarah's hand. "I really need your support."

"Sure," Sarah said.

As Jennifer left, Sarah turned and went back upstairs. She felt good about telling her that she would help with the party. But she'd do it her way. She wasn't going to sneak around—she wouldn't go without checking with her parents first.

In her room she opened up an Alice Walker novel she'd been reading, flipping through to find her place. She heard Tasha's footsteps come to her door, hesitate, and turn away. Then she heard Tasha's guitar. She felt tired and stretched out on her bed, reading slowly.

Sarah rarely dreamed, and when she did it was usually right after a scary movie. Then she would dream about whatever had frightened her in the movie and would wake up in a cold sweat. Whenever that happened she would sit up and read for a while before going back to sleep.

Without the scary movie, she dreamed of being at a huge party. There were thousands of rappers there, and the music was as loud as it could get. She recognized the house first as Jennifer's, and then as her own. Somehow she knew the doorbell was ringing. It was her father coming home and she wanted to tell someone to open the door, only she couldn't shout over the music. She tried and tried and then started to push her way through the crowd of swaying bodies. Someone stopped her, grabbed her by the arm. She tried to fight the person off, and woke in a cold sweat, her hand caught in the blankets. She sat up and turned on the television. An old movie was on. Good, she thought, she was in the mood for something old and familiar.

At school on Monday everybody was buzzing and

whispering. Jennifer and Kwame had their heads together in a corner and Tasha was everywhere.

"Sarah!" Steve Adams took her arm near the water cooler. "Is it true that Jennifer is going to have Def Cru 4 at her party?"

"April told you that?" Sarah was instantly annoyed that April had blabbed to Steve.

"No, does she know about it?" Steve asked.

"Well, who told you?"

"José," Steve said. "You mean it's true?"

"Steve, it's supposed to be a secret," Sarah said.

Steve pulled an imaginary zipper across his mouth and gave Sarah a knowing wink.

The class rotations made today a late-lunch day and Sarah knew there would be a major hubbub. The whole day was going to be a slow drag masquerading as excitement. Jennifer had already given her a note saying that there would be a "conference" at 18 Pine after school.

In the lunchroom Dave was already sitting with Tasha and Cindy when Sarah arrived. They were talking about the Scholastic Aptitude Test, which seemed to be coming up too soon. When Sarah saw Jennifer coming she knew the subject would change.

"What's up, you guys?" Jennifer was almost perking with joy as she sat down in the seat Tasha had saved for her.

"Did you see the lyrics April copied down from

the Cru concert?" Cindy was acting shocked.

"Oh, that," Jennifer said nonchalantly. "It's nothing you haven't heard before."

"Dave's going to bring a copy into English today," Tasha told Jennifer. "This should liven up old Hamlet."

"Uh-oh," Jennifer said slowly. "I don't think Bender had that in mind when she asked for rap lyrics. I think she meant more like Hammer stuff."

"More like Young M.C., you mean," Dave offered.

"Yeah. More, more…mainstream rap," Jennifer said.

"Look, she said she wanted samples. So samples she gets," Dave said flatly. "The third act was getting a little…"

"Tired," Tasha volunteered.

"Very tired," Cindy added.

"I hope this doesn't get you in trouble right before a game, Dave," Sarah offered. Dave hadn't said anything directly to her today, but at least he hadn't left the table when she arrived this time.

"What do you care?" Dave said quietly.

"Excuse me for living," Sarah said.

"Save it," Dave said and looked away.

"Some folks are mighty sensitive today," Sarah said lightly to Cindy.

"And some folks aren't," Cindy whispered back to her. "Chill out."

Billy picked just that moment to come over to their table.

"Slumming today?" Tasha asked him jokingly. He usually sat with a table full of ballplayers and talked sports all during lunch. Now he swung his legs over the chair next to Sarah's and sat down with his tray.

"What's happening?" he asked. "What's up, Dave?" He nodded to Dave, who was starting to pull his things together to leave.

"It's your world, brother," Dave answered evenly. Sarah noticed that he didn't have a trace of hostility in his voice when he spoke to anyone but her.

Jennifer was talking about how rap music was an art form and should be respected. Billy leaned over and asked Sarah if he could see her later.

"What's up?" she asked.

"I got somebody I want you to meet," he said. "Okay?"

Sarah nodded. For some reason, she felt embarrassed.

"I'll see you guys in class," Dave said. He stood to leave.

Sarah wondered what was wrong with Dave. They had been friends for so long and now, suddenly, he hated her.

"I've got to get to the office," Sarah said. "I forgot to sign up for the S.A.T. class."

"When are you taking it?" Cindy asked.

"Soon as I can," Sarah said, balancing her tray on

one hand and carrying her books with the other.

Dave was already pushing his tray through the window to be cleaned. Sarah cut in front of a teacher and pushed her tray through the window.

"Hey, was I just chumped off?" Guy Loving, the music teacher, had a great smile.

"No, Mr. Loving," Sarah said. "I'm just desperate for time. Dave!" she called, trying to sound casual. "Hold up a second, I want to talk to you about something." Sarah caught up with him near the computer room.

He paused in the hallway next to a series of watercolor paintings done by the Art Club. He leaned back against the wall, one hand shoved into his jeans pocket. His dark eyes narrowed as she neared him.

"Why are you so mad at me?" Sarah asked. "What did I do?"

Dave glared at her silently. His eyebrows knitted together and Sarah noticed the slightest twitch starting at the corner of the frown locked on his face. He actually looked quite handsome, she thought.

"Nothing," he said sullenly.

"Dave," she pleaded. "C'mon, what did I do?"

"I said nothing." He looked straight into her eyes.

"Come on, Dave."

"Look, you're just being yourself. And I don't have a problem with that," he paused. "And I'm just being myself, okay, Sarah?" He shoved off of the wall and brushed past her, but Sarah grabbed his arm and swung him toward her.

"Dave, aren't we friends?" Sarah asked. "Haven't we always been friends?"

"Sure," Dave said. "We're friends. You, me, and Billy. Now I have to go to class, okay?"

He walked away, swaggering, saying with his body that he didn't care about a thing in the world. Sarah went back to the cafeteria door and stood there watching him until he turned to go to English. The bell rang and the last-minute rush of students engulfed her.

"Hey, Sarah," Billy said, grinning as he came through the doorway. "You get your S.A.T. review class scheduled?"

"S.A.T. class scheduled?" Sarah remembered that that was the excuse she had used to go after Dave. "Oh, sure, no problem."

"Listen, you fine thing, you." Billy draped an arm over her shoulder. "How about you and me going to Jennifer's party together?"

"I—I don't know if I'm going," Sarah stammered. He had caught her off guard. She didn't realize that Jennifer had started inviting people. "Let me tell you later, okay?"

"I don't want to wait in vain," Billy crooned, doing a Bob Marley accent. "I told Dave we could double-date if he wanted to."

"Oh, good move," Sarah said as they filed into English.

"Okay, class," Mrs. Bender began. "Questions about act three, anyone?"

Not a single hand was raised.

"To be, or not to be?" Robert Thornton, the class clown, finally called out.

"Okay, okay, settle down. I'm glad to see you're all so comfortable with this act that you can quote from it."

Robert stood up and took a bow to the four corners of the room.

"Perhaps Mr. Thornton will do better than anyone else on this little quiz I have prepared for you all," Mrs. Bender said.

Groans were followed by wads of paper flying through the air in the general direction of Robert's head.

"Enough!" Mrs. Bender was all business. "Get out some paper, class. And quietly."

She wrote ten questions on the board. "You have half an hour," she said.

There was silence in the room, broken only by an occasional moan, cough, or a pathetic little whine.

All Sarah could think of was what had probably happened. Billy had told Dave that he was taking her out and Dave was jealous.

"Time," Mrs. Bender called out. "Pass your brilliant reflections on the state of Prince Hamlet's mind to the front of your row, if you will."

Sarah looked at her nearly blank paper, then passed it forward.

"Now then," Mrs. Bender went on, collecting the papers row by row. "I did not forget that we would be looking into contemporary poetry today. I certainly hope that you all remembered as well." She peered out at the class with a twinkle in her eye and slapped their quizzes down on her desk.

"Let's see what we've got here. Who has a rap poem?" She pronounced the words very carefully. "Aaaahhhh, Mr. Hunter." Dave's arm had been the first to go up. "Please stand and read it," she said.

Dave stood and cleared his throat. He had a very serious look on his face.

"What kind of sea is democracy
when it's not clear sailing for you or me
And what kind of trick is this thing called justice
if we stand up for our rights the Man will just bust us?
We try to get ahead and the people push us back
We are the world, and it's our planet
That's my rap and I'm glad I ran it!"

"Well," Mrs. Bender said, gasping a bit. "Thank you, Mr. Hunter. Very strong stuff, yes, class?" She walked around and sat on the edge of her desk.

"Now the, uh, the rhythm. The rhythm, as you'll notice, was very important, was it not?" She looked around the room for agreement. A few students nodded. Some whispered under their breath.

"And the rhyme scheme. What would you say that was, class? Anyone?" She looked around the room for a hand.

"Was it A-A-B-B?" asked a girl near the window.

"Yes, I think so, Lisa," Mrs. Bender answered. She was calmer now. "This was a very political piece, but keep in mind that Hamlet had some political overtones as well. A son at war with his uncle over the throne of his murdered father? Family politics...the destiny, perhaps, of all Denmark..." Mrs. Bender was on familiar turf now.

"And he had a pretty tough rap," Tasha said.

"That he did," Mrs. Bender said, looking satisfied. "Well, I'll check your quiz answers tonight and, since rap is so popular, we'll consider Shakespeare as just another popular communicator."

The bell rang and Mrs. Bender moved aside as the class headed toward the halls.

Billy was standing near the door. Sarah knew he was going to put his arm around her or something stupid. She arranged her books until she was sure Dave had left and then headed toward the door.

"Yo, shall I walk my queen to her next—"

She brushed past Billy quickly. She had made up her mind. It was definitely Dave she liked.

PINE

Nine

What Sarah had wanted to do was to cool out, to stay away from both Billy and Dave until she was ready to deal with them. But she had already promised she would meet Billy at 18 Pine. He had wanted to meet at three, and she told him she couldn't make it before three-thirty.

"So, how's it going?" Kwame plopped down in front of her.

"Kwame, I'm busy," she said.

"Busy? Is that like a dismissal?" Kwame didn't look as if he was going to leave. "Or is that just a busy signal and I should hang up and try again?"

"Kwame." Sarah took a deep breath. She didn't want to talk to Kwame right now, and she didn't want to hurt him, either. "Kwame, do me a favor and just go away. Just for a little bit, okay?"

Kwame held his hands up, palms toward Sarah. He looked around as he stood up to see if anybody had seen her dismiss him. She knew he felt as if she had put him down, but that's the way it was with friends. Nothing was ever serious, and everything was always serious. Sarah had ordered a milkshake, and she moved the straw through it slowly. She looked up and saw that Kwame had sat at the counter.

"Hey, Sarah, how's it going?" Billy stood over her. A girl stood next to him.

"Hi, Billy," Sarah said.

"Look, can I have a word with you?" he asked, beckoning to her.

"Sure." Sarah shrugged, stood up, and moved away from the table.

"Look, Linda, why don't you sit down for a minute?" Billy said to the girl.

The girl sat and Billy pulled Sarah a few steps away. "This is that girl I was telling you about," Billy said.

"And?"

"Maybe you can talk to her," Billy said.

"And say what?"

"I don't know," Billy said. "Maybe tell her what

you were telling me the other day."

Sarah looked past Billy at the girl. She was pretty, with wide, dark eyes and dark brown skin. She had a wide face with a full, sensuous mouth. Sarah could see why any guy would like her.

"Billy, is this your girl?" Sarah asked.

"No, she's just a girl I know," he answered. "I told her that you and I were good friends."

"And you want me to tell this girl that you don't want to marry her?" Sarah said.

"No, all I want you to do is talk to her," Billy said. "She has a lot of problems, and maybe I can't talk to her because we had, like, a boy-girl thing at one time."

"I have a bad feeling about this," Sarah said.

"Look, she doesn't have a lot of money," Billy said. "She can't go to a psychiatrist and she's shy."

Sarah walked over and sat down across from the girl. Out of the corner of her eye she saw Billy go and stand in front of the jukebox with José.

"Hi, I'm Sarah." Sarah offered the girl her hand.

"I'm Linda." The girl tried to smile and then looked away.

"Linda, I don't know what to say to you," Sarah said. "Are you Billy's girlfriend?"

"Yeah," Linda said. "Least I used to be. We broke up. He said that you and he were friends. I asked him if I could meet you."

"Oh?"

"We were going together for a long time," she said. "Then he said that he needed somebody else. He said he outgrew me. I just wondered what you were like."

"Me? Linda, I'm not his girlfriend," Sarah said quickly.

"But you're his friend," Linda said. "And you're someone he likes. So you must be what he wanted me to be."

"You really love him, don't you?"

"I love him a lot." Linda's eyes glistened.

"You want to marry him?"

"I think it would work out," Linda said. "He says he wants to go to college, but I don't mind that. He could go to college and I could work. I'm not, you know, college material or nothing like that."

"You go to Hamilton?" Sarah asked.

"Yeah, see? You can tell, right?"

"No, not right," Sarah said. "I've never seen you at Murphy, so I guessed. Hey, you have the right to love anybody you want. And if you go to college that's fine, but it's fine if you don't, too."

"I love Billy, but I think if he goes to college then I won't stand a chance," Linda said. "He'll meet girls who are going to be doctors and lawyers and I'll be working at Hot Dog King or some place."

"Hey—there's more to your future than that. You can be lots of things. Important things." Sarah took Linda's hands in hers. "If he doesn't realize how great you are..."

"Why don't I just say 'later' to him?"

"Yes," Sarah said. "You seem like such a nice girl, you don't need to run after some guy."

"I thought a lot about this, you know," Linda said. "But there's two things I don't like. One thing is that if he's right, then I got to look around for some boy that's like me. Every time I meet a guy I got to figure out if he's too good for me. That's the first thing."

"Nobody is too good for you," Sarah said. "Everybody doesn't go to college. That's a lot of garbage."

"You going to college?"

"I hope so," Sarah said.

"Okay, the other thing is I feel like he used me," Linda said. "You know, he did what he wanted to do and now he's moving on. I don't feel like I'm just supposed to be used and thrown away."

"You aren't—are you..."

"Pregnant? No. I'm not stupid. But I could have been for all he cared," Linda said. "But girl, you're talking about loving somebody and not loving somebody according to what kind of education and stuff they got. Is that right?"

"I didn't say that!" Sarah said.

"I don't mean you, personally," Linda said. "I mean that's what's behind what Billy's saying."

"Too bad you're not a guy," Sarah said. "You could just punch his lights out."

"Don't you just know it!"

"Hey, that's what I like," Sarah said. "Some good old-fashioned anger. Linda, you need to believe in yourself more. You're too good for Billy—good riddance."

"I got to get on home," Linda said. "Thanks for talking to me. I was just hoping you weren't one of those girls who use fifty-dollar words and make me feel bad. You're real people."

"So are you, Linda," Sarah said. "And if you want to call Billy a few names you can just give me a call and I'll help you. Sarah Gordon, I live on Evergreen."

"My name is Gosset and we're the only Gossets in the telephone book so you can't miss us." Linda stood up. She kissed Sarah on the cheek, smiled, and headed for the door.

"Nice to meet you," Sarah said quietly.

Billy walked Linda outside and to the bus stop. By the time he came back, Sarah had paid for her milkshake and was ready to leave, too.

"Hey, she said you're really nice," Billy said.

"I am," Sarah said.

"And the day is still young," Billy answered, putting on his romantic voice.

"Billy, get a life! You are a world-class creep."

"What did I do?"

"You know what you did," Sarah said between her clenched teeth. "And what you are!"

*　　*　　*

On the way home Sarah thought about Linda and Billy. A year before, Billy had been just another kid playing ball in the schoolyard and singing off-key in the Boys' Chorus. Now he was messing with girls and making decisions that affected other people's lives. Things seemed to be happening so fast to the juniors that it wasn't fair.

Sarah got home, poured a glass of vegetable juice from the gallon jar in the refrigerator, and took it up to her room.

"What's up?" Tasha was in her bathrobe and was munching a carrot when she came into Sarah's room.

"What are you doing in your bathrobe at this time of day?" Sarah asked.

"Allison bet me I couldn't balance a glass of soda on my nose," Tasha answered.

"And naturally you took the bet?"

"Naturally," Tasha answered. "And I spilled it all over myself."

"Brilliant."

"And what's with you?" Tasha asked.

"I'm cool," Sarah answered. She eyed Tasha cautiously. They were sort of getting along. "You looking forward to the party?"

"Sure, I'm looking forward to it. Why shouldn't I?" Tasha challenged her.

"You know, it occurred to me that these guys have to be in their twenties," Sarah said. "Doesn't that bother you?"

"You really think about everything, don't you?" Tasha said. She undid the belt on her robe and retied it. "We haven't had them fingerprinted—you think we should hide the jewels?"

"I'm trying to be responsible," Sarah said.

"Like the way you're being responsible with Billy and Dave?" Tasha asked.

"What are you talking about?"

"What am I talking about?" Tasha bit into her carrot fiercely. "The whole school knows about it. You're supposed to have a thing going with Dave, and then you're making goo-goo eyes at Billy. And they all know that sooner or later Dave and Billy are going to get into a fight over you. You'd like that, wouldn't you? And you're walking around like Little Miss Innocent."

"I can handle my relations with Dave and Billy," Sarah said.

"Right, and Jennifer can handle one night of partying with Def Cru 4," Tasha said.

"You don't even care about her," Sarah said. "You want to have the party and you don't care if she gets in trouble or not."

"Do you care if Dave and Billy fight over you?" Tasha asked.

"Yes, I do," Sarah said. "I really do."

"Well, then you won't mind if I take one of them," Tasha said. "I don't think you'll be much competition. Which one do you want the most?"

"Why don't you get out of my room?" Sarah said.

"Better tell me which one you want," Tasha teased. "Or I'll take both of them."

"Get out of my room, please." Sarah felt her temperature rising. Tasha had pushed the wrong button. "You want to act like a tramp, do it in your own room."

"Sure," Tasha said. "Why not?"

"Tasha, I—" Sarah began. But Tasha had already left.

She wondered if Billy was really leaving Linda for her. She thought he was acting like a creep to the girl he had "used" as Linda had said.

She decided that Billy hadn't left his girlfriend for her. In her heart she wasn't sure, but it was comforting to tell herself that she wasn't to blame.

"Mom, can I talk to you about something?" Sarah asked as they rinsed the dinner dishes.

"About anything, honey," Mrs. Gordon answered. "Is it about Tasha? I wish you two would try and get along."

"No, we're doing okay," Sarah said. "It's about a friend of mine who's giving this party. I don't think she should invite certain people."

"Is she giving it at her house?" her mother asked.

"Yes." Sarah took the glasses from the table and put them into the sink. "I guess so."

"Then it's your friend's responsibility to know who she's inviting and it's the responsibility of the guests to know if they should go there or not. Do you think you should go to this party?"

"No problem for me," Sarah said.

"Then it's probably not much of a problem for your friend, either," her mother said, lining up cups in the dishwasher. "Sarah, there's a thin line between offering friendly counsel and being...well, intrusive."

"Yes, ma'am."

"Not very definite advice, is it?" her mother said.

"I'm beginning to think that after the age of four no advice is too definite," Sarah said.

So that was it. Sarah had made all the decisions she needed. She would help with the salads, she would even go to the party, and afterward she would help clean up. What happened at the party would be Jennifer's problem. The days of Sarah Gordon worrying about what everyone else in the world was doing were definitely over.

When the knock came on the door, Sarah knew it was Allison. Only Allison knocked as if she were the FBI pounding on the door of America's most wanted.

"Allison, is that you?" Sarah asked. "I thought you were off in the Sahara on a Save the Sand project."

"Tasha is kissing a boy outside!" Allison whispered, and pointed girlishly toward the window.

"Then that is none of your business," Sarah said. "And if you snoop I'll tell Daddy."

"Tattletale!" Allison pouted and beat a hasty retreat for her own room.

Sarah made sure her door was closed, turned her lights off, and went to the window. Carefully she pulled down one slat of the venetian blinds. There, in the semidarkness below her window, was a figure standing near the gate. It looked like one rather heavy person until Tasha disengaged herself from Dave Hunter's arms.

Sarah let the blind snap back into place and found her way in the darkness back to her bed. Moments later she heard Tasha's footsteps on the stairs. She closed her eyes and turned her face to the wall, smothering the sound of her crying in her pillow.

PINE

Ten

When Sarah awoke, she was still clutching the small embroidered handkerchief she had taken from her dresser drawer. She looked over at the digital clock radio. It was almost two in the morning. She felt terrible. There was an empty feeling in the pit of her stomach that seemed to draw her into it.

She asked herself what she was feeling. The answer came quickly, easily. It was pain. How could Tasha do this to her? She had deliberately brought Dave back to the house to show Sarah that she could take her man. And Sarah knew she could take Billy, too.

There was a rapping on the window that, for a moment, frightened Sarah. She looked and saw that the wind was rattling the blind. She moved to the window. The sill was wet. Rain was beating relentlessly against the screen. In the distance a low rumble of thunder was followed by a flash of light.

She was still dressed. She switched on her dresser lamp and looked at herself in the mirror. Her hair was matted to one side of her face. She looked a mess.

What to do? What to think? Slink off into the night and feel sorry for herself? Was that what she was supposed to do? Well, she did feel sorry for herself. She didn't even feel angry with Tasha. Tasha was Tasha, and she was Sarah, and in a lot of pain inside.

She went downstairs and leaned against the wall between the kitchen and the hallway. It would be stupid to call anybody this time of night, she thought. It would be very stupid.

She picked up the phone and dialed.

"Hello?" the voice that answered was low, husky.

"Dave?"

"Who is this?"

"Dave, it's me. I'm upset." Sarah spoke softly. Lights from a passing car moved across the kitchen wall, becoming more brilliant as they passed the glass front of Miss Essie's old cabinet. "I'm upset," she repeated.

"Where are you?" he asked.

"I'm home," she said. "I'm hurt because I saw you with Tasha. I guess that's foolish. I mean, I've been so wishy-washy about us. Sometimes I think you care and sometimes…are you still there?"

"I'm still here," Dave said. "I couldn't sleep tonight."

"Dave, can I come to see you?"

"Now?"

"Now. Please." Sarah tried to keep her voice down.

"Hey, it's…" there was a moment of silence. "It's two in the morning. And it's raining."

"Dave…please," Sarah said, holding the phone tightly.

"Look, I'll come over there if you have to see me tonight," Dave said.

"No, I don't want you over here," she said. A vision of Dave and Tasha kissing near the gate flashed through her mind.

"Sure, okay," he said. "Come on."

Sarah went to the hall closet. She took her jacket, slipped it over her shoulders, and started out.

The walk to Dave's house was short, just across the street. How many times had she made it? She had probably even made it in the rain before, she thought.

The rain was cold, almost sleet. Her feet were soaked by the time she reached his house. She went

101

around the back, the way she always did, and saw him standing in the doorway. He opened the door for her and she went in.

"You're soaked," he said.

"It's okay," she said. "It's just a good thing you don't live far away."

He took her wet jacket off her shoulders and she shivered.

"You want a jacket or something?" he asked.

"A blanket would be better," she said.

"Just a minute," he said. He turned and started toward his room, which was down the hall on the first floor.

Sarah followed him. When he had grabbed his blanket from his bed and turned she was there. He swung the blanket around her, holding it open at first and then closing it slowly.

"Look, Sarah." Dave put his arms around her and pulled her close against his chest. "About Tasha..."

"Just tell me if you love her," Sarah said.

"No, I don't," he said. "What happened was..."

Even in the darkness of Dave's room she found his lips, first with her fingertips to silence him, then with her own lips. She didn't want to hear him talk, to fill her head with more words that just seemed to be questions for which she didn't have answers.

He held her for a long while, and for the first time in what seemed like days, she relaxed.

    *   *   *

When she woke she was still wrapped in Dave's blanket. She sat up and saw him sleeping on the floor. By the early morning light she saw that he was using his sneakers for a pillow.

She got up and knelt beside him. "I love you," she whispered softly. She kissed him gently on the cheek as he slept, and started back to her own house.

It was cold, much colder than it had been the night before, but Sarah felt warm. She got home and went quickly up the stairs. She saw the first light of dawn coming through the hall window. It had been a good night, after all.

PINE

Eleven

Sarah avoided Tasha for the next two days, even when she saw her talking to Dave outside the gym at Murphy High. She ached to know what Tasha was saying to Dave, and what he was saying to her. She ached to know, and at the same time she didn't want to know. She felt so many conflicting emotions. She was confident that Dave was through with Tasha, and yet she was still afraid that Tasha's bright smile, the eyes that seemed to flash and dance over his face when she looked at him, would make him turn to her.

Saturday came at last and she was awakened by a

call from Jennifer.

"Can you bring a dip instead of a salad?" Jennifer asked.

"Sure," Sarah said.

"I'm trying to get our crew over to the house by seven to get everything going," Jennifer said. "I think it's really going to be a swinging party."

"When are the guests of honor showing up?"

"Late," Jennifer said. "But that's okay. It'll give us a chance to warm up."

"Okay, I'll be there," Sarah said.

"Can I speak to Tasha?" Jennifer asked.

Sarah called Allison and told her to tell Tasha that Jennifer was on the phone. Allison looked up at the ceiling as if she were really put out. She made a face at Sarah and went off to corral their cousin.

Mrs. Gordon was going shopping and Sarah asked her if she would buy avocados and light cream for the dip. "And can you drop me off at the mall?" she asked.

"Sure," her mother said.

Tasha interrupted her phone call with Jennifer to ask Sarah if she could borrow her red tam. Sarah said that she could, wondering why Tasha wanted it. She thought it was probably her way of breaking the ice.

The drive to the mall was short. Mrs. Gordon asked her daughter how she was doing in school and apologized for not spending more time with her.

"You know, sometimes I find myself so afraid to get into a conflict between you and Tasha that I avoid both of you," she said as she pulled into the drop-off area of the mall.

"I thought it was something like that," Sarah said. "But I appreciate you telling me."

Sarah kissed her mother lightly on the cheek, realized that it was the first time she had kissed her in months, and felt slightly embarrassed.

The mall was full of kids and families going to the early morning breakfast and movie special. Since she had decided to go to Jennifer's party, Sarah thought she should buy a new skirt. She had a white blouse that she hadn't worn, and looked for a skirt to go with it.

She stopped for a moment when she saw a girl who looked like Linda Gosset. It wasn't Linda, but the thought of Linda, who might not be able to get what she wanted in life, bothered her. Sarah pushed Linda from her mind and then felt bad about not thinking about the girl.

She looked at two black silk skirts at Gerson's, decided that neither of them was exactly perfect, and asked the saleswoman to put them aside for her. The saleswoman said she couldn't but didn't think they would be sold if Sarah came back within the hour.

Sarah then went to Ms. Tique, one of the newer shops. They had two black skirts, one that was quite short and the other one longer but with a slit on the side. The slit went high but there was a small band that came with the skirt to put halfway up the leg to hold the slit together if she wanted to. She decided to buy the skirt and use the band. She also bought a pair of super-sheer burnt sienna stockings.

The hours before the party went slowly. She could have made enough dip for the entire East Coast. Finally it was time to go.

"One suggestion." Tasha stood behind her in the bathroom.

"What's that?" Sarah asked.

Without speaking Tasha took the jade pin off Sarah's blouse and put it at the very top of the slit in her skirt. Sarah stood away from the mirror and tip-toed to see how it looked. It looked good.

"Yeah, okay," she said.

Tasha wore Sarah's black beret to which she had added a number of pins, a bright orange t-shirt, and an orange, magenta, and black chiffon skirt that made a swishing noise when she walked. All this color was worn over black tights and low suede boots.

"You both look..." Mr. Gordon searched for the right words, "...lovely."

"Very, er...interesting," Mrs. Gordon commented. "The leather jackets really go nicely with your party clothes."

"We'll get a ride home, okay?" Sarah said. Her mother was driving them to Jennifer's house.

"And we promise to get back at least fifteen minutes before the scandal hits." Tasha added with a grin.

"You girls look so pretty," Miss Essie cooed as she stroked Tarik Jones's fur. The cat looked over the two of them from her lap. Unless there were dangling strings, shoelaces, or loose buttons to play with, he wasn't interested in what they wore.

"Phone us if you need a ride," Mr. Gordon called out as they headed for the car.

They arrived at Jennifer's shortly after seven. Kwame let them in.

"Past your bedtime, isn't it?" Sarah teased him. He was the youngest kid there, but he had the best music collection, so Jennifer had made him disc jockey.

"I'm wide awake now," Kwame grinned, rubbing his hands together. "You two ladies look positively sumptuous." Tasha and Sarah exchanged looks.

"Sumptuous...delectable...entrancing..." Kwame went on. "Am I going over your heads?"

"You're definitely in the deep end of the pool, Kwame. Where's Jennifer?" Sarah was looking around. She wanted to let Jennifer know she was there to help.

"She went up to get dressed about three years ago," Kwame said. "Not a sign of her since. I'm just lining up the music."

"Be right back," Sarah said and went up the stairs

109

to Jennifer's room.

Jennifer opened the door and stood back so that Sarah could see how she looked.

"It looks fine, Jennifer," Sarah said hesitantly. Jennifer was poured into a scoop-necked, low-backed, short black dress with tight lace sleeves. The dress could party by itself.

"Do you think it's too much?" Jennifer asked. "I've got a leather jumpsuit in the closet ready to go."

Sarah sat down on the edge of Jennifer's bed to study her.

"Yeowwwchhh!" Tasha stuck her head in the door. "Girl, you sure you have your fire alarms hooked up?"

"Cut it out, Tasha. Just tell me, is it too much?" Jennifer asked.

"Hey, it's your party, you can slam if you want to." Tasha landed on the bed with a bounce. "This is the room to die for," she said looking around. "Stereo, CD player, television, computer, phone....even a mini-refrigerator. Who says money can't buy happiness?" She fell backward onto the pillows.

Jennifer studied herself in the mirror for a minute. Then she pulled her bathrobe out of the huge closet.

"Okay, why not?" She shot a look toward Sarah and Tasha. "We're all adults here." Sarah turned to give Tasha a warning look, but she was busy checking through Jennifer's CD collection.

110

"Food first, all right?" Jennifer slipped the robe over her dress and led the way to the kitchen. Kwame was still moving furniture in the living room, dancing alone.

"What time is Def Cru 4 getting here?" Sarah asked.

"I'm not sure. Delight kind of moves to his own time, you know?" Jennifer spoke as though she knew him well. "But he's definitely coming!" she added defensively. She nicked her finger opening a can of onion dip, gasped, and licked the cut.

"You okay?" Tasha asked. She was pouring fruit juice into a huge punch bowl.

"Run some cold water on it," Sarah advised. Jennifer seemed nervous and that was making her nervous. They heard the doorbell ring.

Kwame had pushed the dining room table against the wall and was dancing around in there now.

"Oh, hi, babe," Sarah said. She had known Dave would be there, but he had caught her off guard by being early.

"Hi, Tasha." He nodded toward Tasha, all the time putting his arm around Sarah. "You're looking good."

"It's my job," Tasha said.

"What do you want me to do?" Dave asked.

"Ummmm, let me see," Jennifer said. "Could you and Sarah empty that closet by the door? Just dump everything on my mom's bed upstairs. There should be some extra hangers up in her room, too."

"I hope this doesn't involve a lot of heavy lifting," Dave said.

"You want me to test this chicken and make sure it's fresh?" Tasha asked Jennifer. She was dangling a fried chicken leg from her fingers.

"Why don't you go get the hangers, and I'll carry all these coats up," Dave instructed Sarah. She thought about protesting about the division of labor, but decided against it and headed upstairs.

"Now, do you want some help?" she asked when Dave struggled into Mrs. Wilson's bedroom overloaded with coats. She lifted the top half of the pile from his arms. He dumped the rest onto the bed as Sarah, pulled off balance by the weight of the coats, stumbled into him. Jackets and raincoats spilled onto the floor, but Dave managed to grab Sarah and steady her.

"Th-thanks," Sarah barely got out. He was so close that she could feel the warmth of his breath. She looked up into his eyes and a strange feeling of relief washed over her. "Dave, I—" she began. She wanted them to be friends again.

"Ssshhhh," he said softly. He kissed her. "I guess I'm going to have to be cool tonight," he said.

"Try hard," Sarah said.

"Yo, Sar-rahhhh!" Cindy shouted up the stairs. Footsteps in the hall.

"We were—getting the hangers..." Sarah said.

112

She and Dave had made it to the door before Cindy.

"Yeah, right," Cindy teased, checking out Sarah's mussed-up hair, "getting the hang-a what? There is a party going on downstairs, you know."

The place was filling up and Kwame had the music blasting. Sarah and Dave looked at each other.

"I thought you said white sugar was poison," Sarah yelled over the music to Tasha, who was at the table loading desserts onto a paper plate. At least twenty people, some of them strangers to Sarah, were dancing.

"I'm giving the deejay some." Tasha laughed and pointed to Kwame. Then, seeing that she'd gotten chocolate icing on her finger, she licked it off happily. "Dee-lish."

"They're playing our song," Dave informed Sarah. He steered her toward the living room and they inched among the growing crowd of dancers.

Kwame had arranged the music carefully, so that each song was a slight bit faster than the last. As the tempo of the music increased, so did the tempo of the party.

Sarah danced with Dave, with Kwame, and then with José, who she hadn't even known was coming to the party. "I think Jennifer must have invited every boy in Madison over the age of twelve," she said to José as he guided her around Cindy and her partner.

"Check out all the girls here," José said. "This is

just an awesome affair."

Somebody broke in on Kwame's music selection and put on a slow song. Sarah was ready to sit down when she felt strong hands on her waist. It was Dave.

"You have little drops of sweat on your eyebrows," he said.

"It must be two hundred degrees in here," Sarah answered, trying to reach under his arm to wipe away the sweat.

"Don't wipe it off," he said. "They look like jewels."

"Wow, that's so poetic," Sarah said, snuggling closer.

"I read it in a book," Dave said.

Sarah gave him a poke for spoiling the illusion, then relaxed in his arms, letting the rhythm of their bodies lead them around and through the music. She felt she could slow-dance with him forever, but all too soon the song had ended and another took its place.

"You and Dave look so-o-o good together," Tasha said as she pulled a reluctant Steve Adams into the middle of the floor. "A perfect couple."

Sarah looked at her, surprised at the remark.

Tasha shrugged, and shrugged again, making each shrug somehow sexier and cuter as she moved her shoulders to the rhythm of the reggae beat. Soon some of the other dancers were trying to imitate her.

The girl could dance. Her body was fluid, and the music seemed to lift her and carry her along.

"She's just great!" Sarah said.

"Yeah, she's okay," Dave said, holding her tighter.

Sarah wondered what she had ever worried about. The party was going great guns. It didn't matter if Def Cru 4 showed or not.

She looked out on the floor. It was a brilliant rainbow of colors whirling together, though the driving pulse of the music almost tore it apart.

"I've died and gone to heaven!" Jennifer said, shouting inches from Sarah's face to make herself heard.

Sarah thought she smelled liquor on Jennifer's breath, then pushed the idea out of her mind. It was Jennifer's party, as Tasha said. She could slam if she wanted to.

Nobody on the far side of the room or out on the deck could hear the doorbell, even when the room wasn't rocking with sound. But somebody near the door must have heard the knocking and when the door opened a buzz filled the room. Def Cru 4 had arrived.

Sarah saw Jennifer tug at her dress and run her hands over her hair. A scream of laughter came from the kitchen.

"Hi! Join the party!" she called out, moving toward the door. This was it. They were actually here.

Delight came in first. He was wearing a black cape and carrying a lacquered walking stick. Jennifer rushed to him.

"Oh, yeah, there you are." Delight came toward her. The girl hanging from his arm had on a fringed suede halter top that showed off most of her chest.

"Get me some liquid, baby," Delight crooned to the girl. He patted her bottom and sent her off.

"Okay, okay. We're going live, right, Jennifer?" Kwame's voice boomed over the microphone. A chair creaked loudly in the dining room. Someone was standing on it to get a better look over the heads in the room. One of the guys from the football team, whose name Sarah forgot, dimmed the lights.

"Yeah," Jennifer called back.

"Tell 'em, sweet thing," said a guy standing behind Delight. Up close the Def Cru 4 group looked as if they must be even older than their twenties.

Delight grabbed the microphone from Kwame. The party erupted into cheers, then Delight smiled and yelled, "Party time!"

"Let's do it." Jennifer took Delight's hand and started dancing in the middle of the floor.

The general dancing began again, but everyone had an eye on Def Cru 4. Sarah counted nine of them, seven guys and two girls. Two of them were leading a procession of dancers out onto the deck.

The party was getting wilder by the moment, led by Jennifer herself. She danced with Delight, and then with two other guys from the group. Sarah noticed that they had their hands all over her.

"Fly girl, you want to dance?"

He was tall and thin and had dreads that seemed to sprout from his head like petals from African violets. He danced so smoothly that Sarah felt as if he were just an extension of herself.

"We can't stay too long, baby," he said. "So maybe we can get something going in a little bit?"

Sarah smiled as prettily as she could, and said, "I don't think so."

"You uptight or something?" he asked.

"I'm here with my boyfriend," Sarah said.

The guy looked as if he was almost thirty. He could dance, but Sarah was glad when the music stopped and he moved quickly away from her to another girl.

There was something going on in the kitchen, and Sarah asked Dave if he knew what it was.

"They're in there drinking," Dave said. "And whatnot."

"What is whatnot?" Sarah asked.

"I didn't stay in there long enough to find out," Dave said.

The party had gone from noisy and jumping to a kind of frenzy. One of Def Cru 4's members, an intense, muscular-looking guy, said something to Kwame and Kwame shook his head. The guy pushed Kwame away pretty hard.

"I think we're at the fifteen-minute point, time to make evacuation arrangements," Tasha yelled into Sarah's ear.

The floor was actually throbbing. Dave's steady arms held her around the waist. She could leave anytime now.

Tasha was leaning back against José, who was perched on a stool. José made a gesture Sarah didn't understand, but Tasha seemed to. Climbing off his stool, he took Tasha gently in his arms. Together they waltzed slowly around the room. So out of time were they with the rap that was shaking the house that they were followed by laughter wherever they danced. The same guy who had pushed Kwame cut in, and glowered at José.

There was a crash and Sarah looked to see a lamp in pieces on the floor. Jennifer started toward it and Delight took her wrist and brought her back to the dance floor.

"Things are getting nasty," Dave said. "You want to split?"

"I don't know. I don't want to leave Jennifer," Sarah said. "But yeah—I'm going to call my father."

Dave led her through the crowd, using his athletic skills to ward off the bodies. The kitchen was full of the smell of incense and sweat. Sarah found the phone and dialed quickly.

"Hello, Daddy, come and get us. It's pretty bad over here!" she said. "Can you come right away?"

18

PINE

Twelve

"You live here?" The two police cruisers arrived at the same time as Mr. Gordon.

"My daughter is at this party," Mr. Gordon said.

"We got three complaints in the last half hour." The younger policeman, a little under six feet and compactly built, looked over Mr. Gordon carefully. "You stay out here, buddy," he said, then turned to one of the other officers and indicated that he should keep an eye on Mr. Gordon.

José opened the door and stepped back, wide-eyed, when he saw the police officers.

Sarah saw the two officers enter just as screams of

laughter came from the kitchen. She elbowed her way in that direction. A girl was in the downstairs bathroom, with the door open, throwing up in the toilet bowl. For the most part, she had missed her target.

There was a loud crash, followed by screams. Sarah froze. She didn't want to know what happened.

"Somebody shut that music off!" one of the policemen yelled.

"Oh, my god! Jennifer, it's the deck!" Cindy had run to the window and was staring out at the back of the house. Her face was contorted by shock. Sarah looked out the window to see that the railing around the deck had been ripped from its foundation.

The police assembled everyone in the living room and started sorting out the mess.

The Def Cru 4 band got a personal police escort to their van, but Delight had stopped long enough to tell Jennifer that her party stank.

On the way home it was Tasha who cried. She was in the back of the car with Cindy and Sarah, while Dave and José were in the front seat with Mr. Gordon.

Mr. Gordon drove José home first, then swung back toward the Gordon's neighborhood and dropped off Cindy, and then Dave before finally pulling into the Gordon driveway.

They sat in the car for a minute before he spoke. "You ladies have some explaining to do."

Tasha didn't say anything. Sarah waited a second, then quietly said, "You and Mom have been telling me that I worry about other people's lives too much, that people have to have the freedom to live their own lives. I told Mom I was worried about the party, but she said it wasn't my business."

Mr. Gordon lost his cool for just a second. "Young lady," he said, then caught his breath. "Your mother told me about your conversation. And you're right. To a point. But you never told her that the party was unchaperoned. You crossed the line." He paused and then looked at Tasha. "Tasha, Mrs. Gordon and I have given you a lot of slack since you arrived. That was probably our mistake. If you're going to live under our roof, you need to live by our rules. One of those rules is that you tell us where you're going, and who's going to be there. Is that clear?"

"Yes, sir." Tasha was clearly upset. She glanced at Sarah, who gave her a small smile that said they were in this together.

Everyone was up. Miss Essie had made tea and Allison was in her bathrobe and slippers.

"Is everyone okay?" Mrs. Gordon asked.

"Yeah," Mr. Gordon nodded. "They looked out for each other fairly well."

"I'm so sorry," Tasha said. "Sarah said it was

121

going to be too wild a party. I should have listened to her."

"What exactly happened?" Miss Essie asked.

"Jennifer gave a party for the juniors," Tasha said. "She wanted to make it a swinging party. She thought—I guess a lot of us thought—that if she invited Def Cru 4 it would really be a blast."

"And?" Mrs. Gordon asked.

"And the rappers got wild," Tasha said. "They started pushing people around. They brought liquor and who knows what else with them."

"Anybody get hurt?" Allison asked.

"Just some twisted ankles and a few bruised egos," Tasha said.

"And a lot of furniture," Sarah said. "A lot of furniture."

Sarah was up by nine the next morning. Her new skirt was lying in a heap in the corner and the rest of her clothes were piled on the chair. She got up and went to the bathroom. Her mouth felt as if it were home to a collection of lint balls.

She brushed her teeth, went back to her room and dressed in jeans, and went downstairs. Her parents were sitting at the table. Allison was lying on the floor, reading the Sunday comics. When she saw Sarah she looked away, a sure sign that her parents had been talking about her.

"Sarah," her mother said in the hesitating way she

had when she was troubled, "perhaps we should have a talk."

"I'm sure we should have a talk," Sarah said. "I know I deserve a talk. But right now I would love a lift over to Jennifer's house to see how she's doing."

"Why don't you just call her?" her father suggested.

"I think I want to talk to her in person," Sarah said. "I feel really responsible for what happened last night. At least partially responsible."

"You had told me that you were troubled about the party, Sarah. I'm sorry I didn't take the time to talk with you about it," her mother added. She glanced at her husband and then back at Sarah.

"Would you give me a lift, Dad?"

"Yeah, sure."

They drove to Jennifer's house in almost complete silence. Her father said he didn't know what to say, and simply didn't say any more.

Jennifer was standing in the doorway when Sarah kissed her father and headed up the path.

"Hi, friend." Sarah stopped a few yards away from Jennifer. "How you doing?"

"Hi, Sarah," Jennifer answered cheerily. "How are you doing?"

"Jenn, I'm really sorry about last night."

"It wasn't your fault," Jennifer said. "Come on in. You want coffee?"

"You got orange juice?" Sarah looked around the

living room. It was a mess. There was food every-where, and the broken lamp pieces were still on the floor. Some books were scattered in front of the televi-sion. They seemed to be covered with some kind of dark liquid.

"I haven't even cleaned the bathroom," Jennifer said. "And you know how that looked last night."

"Was there much damage?"

"The lamp was a Tiffany, about sixteen hundred, the rug will take a hundred or so to clean, the deck rail another eight hundred," Jennifer said. "The Depres-sion glassware was probably worth a good three thou-sand."

"You're in deep you-know-what!" Sarah said.

"I couldn't even face my mom," Jennifer said. "I called my dad and he said he'd take a commuter flight from Providence. I thought that was him when you drove up. Look, I appreciate your dropping by like this."

"No problem," Sarah said. "Look, let's see if we can get this place into shape."

"No can do," Jennifer said. "The sink is stopped up in the kitchen. I'm not hauling water from the base-ment and the bathroom is too nasty to deal with on an empty stomach. I thought I'd start by getting the sink unstopped."

The doorbell rang.

"My father," Jennifer said.

"Be brave," Sarah said. "I'll start the explanations."

Sarah hadn't seen Mr. Wilson in a number of years, but she knew that the thin woman with the too wide grin and the streaked blond wig was definitely not him. She opened the door and put an inquisitive look on her face.

"Yes?"

"Oh, I'm Shawnee," the woman said. "I'm Jennifer's friend."

"Oh." Sarah stepped aside and let her in. "Jennifer! It's your friend—it's your friend—what did you say your name was?"

"Where's Dad?" Jennifer asked from behind Sarah.

"He got tied up and thought"—Shawnee nodded as she looked around the house—"and thought that this might be a chance for us to get to know each other better."

"Sarah, this is my father's girlfriend," Jennifer said. "Isn't she special?"

"We were just unstopping the sink," Sarah said. "You know anything about plumbing?"

"Plumbing?" Shawnee smiled her wide smile and shook her head.

"Well, maybe you can clean the bathroom while Jennifer and I work on the plumbing," Sarah said.

"I thought maybe we could just talk about what happened," Shawnee said.

"You going to give me some motherly advice?" Jennifer asked.

"Perhaps I should just take a look at the damage and tell your father," Shawnee said curtly.

Jennifer bowed and gestured for Shawnee to look around.

"This is my father's girlfriend," Jennifer said quietly to Sarah. "He went out and found this pitiful creature and had the nerve to tell me that he was thinking seriously of marrying it."

"She's only twenty-five?" Sarah asked.

"If you add her physical age to her mental age it doesn't add up to my father's age, which is forty-four," Jennifer said. "It does, however, add up to her IQ. Her full name is Shawnee Cunningham."

Shawnee looked around the house, stopped at the stairs until Jennifer gestured for her to go up, and then nervously went to the second floor.

When she came down she asked Jennifer if she was sure she didn't want to talk about it.

"No," Jennifer said. "I don't want to talk about it, Miss Cunningham."

"Then I guess I'll be headed back to Providence," Shawnee said. "It's not really as bad as all that, is it?"

After Shawnee left, Sarah turned to Jennifer and said, "I think she's afraid of you, Jennifer. It's not her fault that she's young and stupid, you know."

Jennifer shrugged, "I know. But she gets me so angry—I just didn't want her hanging around."

Sarah went to the kitchen sink and saw that it was

half filled with water. "You want to try a coat hanger?" she asked.

"Why not?"

They found a coat hanger and worked for five minutes until they fished out a necktie.

"The question," Sarah said, "is whether someone is down there trying to pull himself out. Jennifer…" She put her arm around her friend.

"You're allowed one 'I told you so' and one 'tsk tsk,'" Jennifer said.

"Last night, I just couldn't tell if you were having a good time or if you were having a miserable time," Sarah said.

"Neither." Jennifer flopped down on a chair. "I was just having a time. When I went to visit my father the last time and saw him with this chick, I guess I just flipped out. At first I just told myself the whole thing was cool. You know, it's man's nature to want a woman, that kind of thing. And why not a woman who's just a few years older than me?"

"You feel like doing any serious boo-hooing, you go right ahead," Sarah said.

"No, I've done all of that," Jennifer said. She picked up a glass containing a mysterious liquid and brought it to her nose.

"What is it?" Sarah asked.

"Industrial-strength industrial waste," Jennifer said. "Anyway, then I started feeling bad about the whole thing. Somewhere in between feeling that it was okay and that it was terrible, I decided that the problem was that I wasn't acting adult enough to handle the whole bit."

"And so you were going to start being as adult as you needed to be?" Sarah said. "And Def Cru 4 was going to be the start?"

"You want to hear the seduction scene I had planned for Delight?" Jennifer asked.

"Why is it that everything that Allison thinks is adult has something to do with her wearing my clothes," Sarah said, "and everything that we think of doing that's adult has to do with sex?"

"You tell me!"

"Look, let's do something very adult," Sarah said. "Let's get the gang over here and clean this place up."

"I don't know if I can face them, Sarah," Jennifer said.

"If I know our crowd they won't be able to face themselves if they don't help," Sarah said. "I'll make the calls. You start on the bathroom."

"Couldn't we get a sophomore over for that?" Jennifer asked, smiling.

Sarah threw her a towel and headed for the phone.

Thirteen

Dave Hunter's mother was funny. She was all excited because Sarah had dropped by. She made a tray of cookies from dough that came in a tube.

"You want anything else?" she asked Sarah.

"No, Mrs. Hunter, these are really nice," Sarah said.

"You should have told me you had them hidden away," Dave said.

"And let you eat them all?" Mrs. Hunter threw a dishtowel at her son.

Dave caught the towel in one hand and folded it neatly near his tray.

"I'll be upstairs if you want anything, honey," she said to Sarah.

"Your mother's sweet," Sarah said when Mrs. Hunter had left. "This is so nice and old-fashioned."

"You should have seen what she would have broken out with if she had known you were coming," Dave said. "That was great the way you helped Jennifer get the cleanup crew together this morning."

"You have that many girls coming over here?" Sarah asked.

"You know I don't," Dave said. He had been sitting on the piano bench and got up and crossed to where Sarah was sitting on the couch and put his arm around her. "I'm glad you're here now, though," he said.

He kissed her on the cheek. He turned her head and kissed her again, ever so gently, on the lips.

She stood and crossed to the piano bench where he had been sitting.

"We going to play tag?" Dave asked.

"I think we should talk," Sarah said.

"Sure."

"Look, this might sound a little confusing, but I think maybe we should cool out for a while." Sarah looked down at her palms. "You know, I was talking to Linda the other day—do you know her?"

"The girl Billy used to go with?"

"Yes," Sarah said. "He wanted to break off their relationship and he wanted me to help him."

"I don't get that," Dave said. "You interested in going with him?"

"No, I'm not," Sarah said firmly. "I let him talk to me because, and only because, you didn't seem interested. Then he tried to use me to break off from Linda. She's a nice girl, really. He gave her a line about not being good enough for him. Then I was supposed to represent what was good enough for him, I guess."

"Hey, where do I fit into all of this?" Dave asked.

"Well, at first I was mad at Billy when I saw that he had just used Linda and was ready to dump her and move on," Sarah said. "Then I was mad at him for trying to use me to get rid of her. Then I felt bad for Linda, because she wasn't in control of her situation. Then I was mad at Def Cru 4 for the way I think they tried to use us at the party. All they saw were a bunch of kids they thought they could walk on."

"They did a pretty good job of it, too," Dave said.

"But mostly I'm mad at me. I realize now that the reason I've been chasing Billy down the halls of Murphy High is because I need to be needed. When our relationship cooled off after the Big Auction Weekend, I felt alone and afraid. And I decided that finding somebody was a good idea. And it wasn't."

"You know, you've got me up and down on a string like I'm a toy or something," Dave said. "Doesn't what I want count in this?"

"Sure." Sarah looked directly into his eyes. "Sure it does. Dave, please understand. Your friendship means everything to me. But you're you and I'm me and I have to decide what's best for me. I think, in a lot of ways, that's what makes this junior year so hard. We have to make so many decisions. If we're going to college, what college we're going to. What we're going to do with our lives. What we're going to do with our bodies."

"And you've decided to put yours in cold storage?" Dave asked.

"I've decided to put it in cold storage for today, and to keep thinking about it seriously," Sarah said. She knew she needed Dave to get through this part of her life, and she wanted him as a friend. The way he'd always been.

"And you came all the way over here to tell me this?"

"I came over here to hear me say it, I think," Sarah said. "And to hope you wouldn't be mad at me. I really want to be friends. I need you so much."

There was a silence that hung between them like a fog. Sarah started to get up to leave, but her legs didn't move. Dave was leaning forward, his chin in his hands. She hoped he would say the right thing, so that she could feel good about what she had said.

They heard his mother's footsteps in the hall and both sat up straight.

Dave smiled. They hadn't been doing anything,

but they had been caught having a very special moment together, and they both realized it.

"I'd better be going," Sarah said.

"You going to be at 18 Pine this week?"

"Where else?"

"Then I guess I'll see you there, buddy," he said. He put his arms around her and held her for a long moment. Sarah was so happy she almost cried.

"You know, this wasn't as bad as I thought it would be," Jennifer said, adjusting her apron.

"Yes, it was," Tasha said.

"But I dealt with it," Jennifer said. "I just never thought I'd see the mall from the wrong side of the counter."

"I had the hardest job," Sarah said.

"Well, this was your idea, Sarah Gordon," Tasha said. "You deserved to be our fearless leader."

"It was only right!" Sarah insisted.

"Nobody said it wasn't, cuz," Tasha said. "But that doesn't mean I'm going to let you enjoy it."

It had been Sarah's idea for them to help pay for the damages to Jennifer's house. It wasn't that easy getting short-term jobs on short notice, but they had finally found them. Mrs. Wilson had agreed that five hundred dollars would be sufficient, even though the damages had been a lot more. One day's work by all the crew from 18 Pine St. would just about make it.

Dave and Billy did inventory at Worth's and

Kwame found a job scrubbing a laundromat. Steve and José spent a day working for Steve's father. Only Cindy and April weren't working. Cindy had come down with a killer cold and April hadn't been to the party.

Sarah, Tasha, and Jennifer had found a one-day job filling in at a local diner.

The girls had arrived at Al's Deluxe Diner at twelve-thirty and had worked through dinner. It had been a hard day. The restaurant would close in a few minutes.

"When I get home the first thing I'm going to do is to scratch 'waitress' off my list of favorite jobs," Jennifer said.

"Jennifer, you're a lousy waitress," Sarah said. "I just want to share that with you."

"I am not!"

"When a customer asks for another cup of coffee you can't say no!" Tasha said.

"He already had two cups," Jennifer said. "And my feet were killing me. And not only that, but he kept calling me 'baby.'"

"I can't believe it," Tasha said. "Look at these people."

They watched as three people stood outside the diner and read the menu Al had posted on the front door. "If they come in I'm going to have a fit!"

"I thought Al said the place closed at exactly seven," Sarah said.

"It closes at seven but you can't kick the people out who are already here," Tasha said.

"Can you try?" Jennifer asked.

There were only two customers in the restaurant, and they were almost finished eating. The door swung open and the three came in, and Al greeted them at the door.

"Tasha, tell them the food is lousy," Sarah said.

Tasha pushed herself off her chair and made her way over to the table where the two women and a man were sitting.

"Table two is leaving," Jennifer said.

Sarah got her tray and went over to the table. She stacked the dishes on the tray, put the eighty-five cents they had left for a tip near the sugar bowl, and wiped the table down.

One of the things she didn't like about being the busgirl was that after she cleaned the table, one of the waitresses would get the tip. She didn't mind it for the other waitresses, only when she had to clean up tables for Tasha and Jennifer. She turned and looked at the clock on the wall. Two minutes to seven.

"Why don't you girls sit down and have a nice cup of coffee for yourselves?" Al said, smiling. "Soon as the last customers leave we all pitch in and clean up and then we're out of here!"

Sarah took her dishes to the kitchen. The dishwasher looked up from his *Racing Form* long

135

enough to give her a dirty look and point to the trash can.

Sarah held her breath while she scraped the dishes into the can, then put them on the counter.

Tasha came into the kitchen.

"Did you tell them the food was lousy?" Sarah asked.

"Yeah, but then I made the mistake of telling them we had ketchup and they said it was fine," Tasha moaned.

Table five seemed to be settling in for a long conversation when Sarah sat down with Jennifer.

"My shoulders are so tired I can't lift my arms to scratch my nose," Sarah said.

"My feet hurt!" Jennifer said. "Even sneakers hurt when you've been standing all day."

Tasha took sodas to her customers and came back and flopped down next to Jennifer.

"You know, if I died right now I'd go straight to heaven," she said. "I mean, who could deny my suffering?"

"Hey, I want to tell you guys how much I appreciate this," Jennifer said. "I mean, I don't want to get drippy or anything, but I appreciate it."

"I thought your mom was going to have a fit," Tasha said. "She wasn't too bad, really. She understood the whole thing was just about having a party and no one meant to tear the place up."

"No, it wasn't about having a party," Sarah said.

136

"I think it was about Jennifer's father's girlfriend."

"Sarah, shut up!" Tasha said. "You got your way with us all working and everything, don't go making like a junior psychiatrist or something."

"She's right, though." Jennifer nodded. "You want sodas?"

"I'll get them," Tasha said. "No, I think I won't, I'm too tired."

Jennifer got up and went behind the counter to the soda dispenser.

"You know, I don't like the way you tell me to shut up," Sarah said. "One of these days I'm going to slap you silly."

"Sarah, the day you lift your hand to me will be the day you lose your hand and your life." Tasha pointed her finger at Sarah.

"Don't put your hands in my face!" Sarah said.

"Will you two cool out!" Jennifer put the sodas down. "You're worse than old married people."

"Look at table five, putting his cigarette out in his coffee cup," Tasha said. "Slob!"

"Sarah was right about the party being about Shawnee," Jennifer said. "Or at least partially about her."

"What happened when you went to Providence?" Tasha asked.

"First thing, I was surprised to see her," Jennifer said. "I just imagined my father as always being, you know, my father. I liked to think about him working, or sitting around being cool. When I saw Shawnee—"

"Is she part Cherokee or something?" Tasha asked.

"I don't know where she got that name," Jennifer said. "I don't think she's part Native American, though. Anyway, when I first saw her, I immediately went into a mental thing, like, why shouldn't my father have a girlfriend? Then I saw that it wasn't just a girlfriend, that he was serious about this woman. Then, of course, I found everything about her that I didn't like. I still don't like her."

The bell rang, signaling that Tasha's order was ready. "Don't say anything juicy until I get back," she said.

"You know you don't have to talk about it," Sarah said when Tasha left.

"It's either talk about it or have another party," Jennifer said.

Tasha made two trips to the kitchen before she came back. Table five left and Al cleaned the table.

"He'd better not take my tip," Jennifer said.

Tasha came back with a funny look on her face. "Don't look over there," she said. "But the woman in the green dress ordered creamed corn. I brought it over and she tasted it and said it wasn't fresh, and that I should take it back. I took it back and gave it to the cook. He put some butter in it, stuck it in the microwave for two seconds, and gave it

138

back to me. She loved it."

"After today, I'm giving up eating anyway," Sarah said.

"So you don't like her?" Tasha asked.

"I just don't like the idea that everything is really final now," Jennifer said. "It's like my parents were divorced, but they were really just having an argument. You know what I mean?"

"Yes, I think so," Tasha said.

"So I felt that I was being juvenile about the whole thing," Jennifer said. "I had to accept things the way they were, not the way I wanted them."

"And having the party, a real knock-down bash, was showing how you accepted things?" Tasha asked.

"Does it make any sense?" Jennifer asked.

"I think so," Sarah said.

"If it makes sense to our junior psychiatrist here, then it makes sense," Tasha said.

"Do you two dream about fighting each other?" Jennifer asked.

"Sometimes," Sarah said. "Sometimes."

Mrs. Gordon picked them up. Jennifer took her shoes off in the back of the car and put her feet up.

"Rough day?" Mrs. Gordon asked.

"No," Tasha said. "We've all decided to drop out of Murphy tomorrow. We've just found our spot in life. Al's Deluxe Diner."

"What was the worst thing that happened?" Mrs. Gordon asked.

"When I found out that when Al cleaned my last table for me he snatched my tip," Jennifer said. "It's a cold world out there, Mrs. G., believe me."

Mrs. Gordon asked Sarah how her day had been, but her daughter was already asleep.

Fourteen

"Has anybody heard Allison's presentation?" Mr. Gordon asked.

"She wouldn't let anybody hear it," Tasha said. "It was all hush-hush in her room. Just her and Pamela working away up there."

They were at the Westcove Mall. Mr. Gordon had driven Allison and Pamela over to enter the Third Annual Save the Earth Day Competition. Sarah and Tasha had come to see what Allison was going to do, and Kwame Brown had entered the contest himself.

"Kwame did this neat project," Tasha said. "A whole thing about the ozone layer. He's got charts, pictures from the government, everything."

"This kind of competition is excellent," Mr. Gordon said. "Young people should be aware of what is and isn't good for the environment."

"Spoken like a true teacher, Uncle Donald," Tasha said.

"He's right," Sarah said. "By teaching the really young kids about the earth we can keep up their enthusiasm."

"Oh, he's right," Tasha mimicked Sarah. "We're so protective of our fathers. Are you going to give a party, Sarah?"

"What's that mean?" Mr. Gordon asked.

"Oh, nothing, Dad," Sarah said.

There were nearly fifty kids in the exhibition. One had constructed a model of the earth that looked fairly realistic.

"But it doesn't do anything," Tasha said.

The kids went up on a stage, one by one, to explain their projects. There were three exhibits showing how fur trappers were cruel to animals. Two showed the cycle of carbon dioxide and oxygen production over the rain forests, and one predicted the dread consequences of global warming.

"I should have done something more spectacular." Kwame had come over when he saw the Gordons. "I think I'm the only one with a paper."

"It's supposed to be Save the Earth Day," Sarah said, "not art projects."

"Is there a prize or something?" Tasha asked.

"Everybody who enters a project gets two tickets to the theater," Kwame said. "And the top three get portable CD players."

"Made out of nonbiodegradable plastics," Tasha said.

"There's Allison and Pamela. I think they're on next," Tasha said. "Wave to them so they'll see us."

Sarah, Kwame, and Tasha stood and waved and Allison waved back.

"Their timing is perfect," Tasha said. "There's the television crew just setting up."

The boy who was showing off his project was demonstrating how to turn leaves into mulch and giving out dire warnings about the dangers of burning them. The television crew was set up and the people around it were watching the small monitor the crew had set up instead of the boy himself. Then Allison and Pamela came on.

They had struggled with the large box that contained their project, even insisting on carrying it to the car themselves. They hadn't given a clue as to what it was, or why it smelled vaguely like grape soda. Allison did the talking as Pamela dramatically lifted the box.

"Ladies and gentlemen, and boys and girls," Allison started with a huge smile. "We are talking about the need to start a worldwide program for gum control!"

Sarah put her hand over her eyes, then opened her fingers just wide enough to see the huge ball of chewed-up gum that Allison and Pamela had brought as their project.

"This ball of chewed-up gum represents just the work of two girls, me and Pammy," Allison was saying. "But we figured out that when we started this project just two weeks ago, there were one hundred and four million kids in the United States alone who might have been chewing gum. Since Pammy and I are two people we divided the number in two, which made fifty-two million balls.

"Now, if all those balls of chewed-up gum were spread all over the country it would be a mess! You couldn't go anywhere without stepping on gum. And if animals ate it they would get everything from fur balls if they were cats to shrimp balls if they were dolphins. And I don't know how long gum can last but I saw some gum on a friend's bed that was there over three years, so you see we desperately need gum control before it is too late!"

There was a smattering of light applause and then a heavy man raised his hand to ask a question. "What would happen if a bird ate that gum?" he asked.

Allison didn't say anything—she just grabbed her throat and keeled over. Obviously she didn't think much of birds eating gum.

There was more applause and laughter and the

next exhibitors came up on the platform, giving a wide berth to the super-wad of grape gum.

Sarah smiled as she thought about her sister. Sometimes it was hard to tell whether she was the smartest eleven-year-old of all time, or whether the lights were on and nobody was home.

PINE

Fifteen

"Yo! Yo! Yo!" April came bopping into 18 Pine St. She was wearing a Los Angeles Raiders cap with the bill turned backward, and tiny sunglasses.

"What are you doing, pal?" Sarah watched as April went all around their table.

"Yo! Yo! Yo!" April stopped and started going in the opposite direction.

Jennifer grabbed her jacket and held her in one spot but she kept bobbing her head as if she were still strutting.

"This is Earth, calling April!" Tasha called. "April, please come in!"

"Check this out," April said. "I think I'm going to start my own rap group. I'll call it Light Ice. What do you think?"

"Why?" Sarah asked.

"Then again, why not?" April answered. "Mrs. Bender said rap was a form of modern poetry, right?"

"Mrs. Bender will say anything to get us reading poetry," Sarah said.

"Okay, maybe, but it still is," April said. "But maybe we can take rap and do some really great things. We can even rap an opera!"

"No!" Tasha said. "I am not going to rap an opera!"

"Well, who's willing to go in on this thing with me?" April asked.

"If anybody goes in on it with you they'll probably be arrested for impairing the morals of a minor," Jennifer said.

"No, no, you don't get it," April said. "It'll be clean, friendly rap."

"A kinder, gentler rap," Sarah said. "April, why don't you get into something useful, like saving whales or something?"

"All the good things are taken, now that gum control is gone," April said.

"I feel personally disgraced that two little girls with a big wad of chewed-up gum should get one of the top prizes and the marvelous Kwame did not," Kwame said. "Plus they got their disgusting little project on the news."

148

"I think they just put it on television because it was cute," Jennifer said. "I mean, I don't really believe that gum is a world danger."

"You don't know that," Tasha said. "I mean, I've seen gum stuck under desks in schools that looks like Abraham Lincoln might have chewed it. Do you think it ever goes away?"

"And what does happen if it goes into the ocean?" Sarah said. "Allison has this whole theory about how it's going to kill all the mammals."

"Is she really worried?" April asked.

"No, I think she's moved on to something else now," Tasha asked. "I saw her and Pamela taking balls of string into her room. So they've either got a new project going or they're finally going to take care of Sarah once and for all. I think they could have had their gum wad get her."

"Hey, wait a minute." Kwame raised his hand. "We're supposed to be taking over the world in a few years, and here we are talking about chewed-up gum and trying to figure out if we want to start a new rap group. When are we going to get to the serious stuff?"

"Like what?" Sarah asked.

"Like world peace," Kwame said.

"Well, go on, Kwame Brown," Jennifer said. "Tell us about world peace."

"I think we should all concentrate on world peace," Kwame said. "What we need to do is to embrace the peace movement ourselves to demonstrate how easy it is. And since I brought the subject up I'll start by embracing Tasha here. Then I'll move right down the line—" He moved his chair closer to Tasha's.

"Whoa!" Jennifer held up her hand. "Kwame, you are still the same sorry example of wasted youth that you have always been. Do something useful, boy. Take this seven dollars, which represents all I have left of my allowance, and see if you can exchange it for pizza."

"If you insist," Kwame said, taking the money. "Extra everything?"

"Naturally," Jennifer said.

"Wait for me, Kwame, I'll get the sodas," April said.

"You're not going to stay for the fight?" Tasha asked.

"What fight?" April asked.

"I had a man who was going to embrace me and Jennifer just bought his affections right from under my nose," Tasha said. "That definitely calls for a fight!"

"All right!" April stood and put her hat back on.

"The girl's going to fight
For what she thinks is right
And that's a man that's fine
at 18 Pine!"

"April! April! April!" The gang cheered and applauded. "Now go for the sodas."

Don't miss Book 3, The Prince

"Are you to be the fair Juliet?" Ibrahima asked.

"We haven't really thought that far ahead," Cindy answered.

"She'll probably be our Juliet," Sarah said. "You want to play Romeo?"

"I'm afraid I couldn't," Ibrahima said. "No one in my line can do anything that might bring disfavor to the throne." He kissed Cindy's hand and left.

"I think we'll be seeing more of the gentleman," Sarah said. "What do you think, Juliet?"

"Who can think at a time like this?" Cindy asked. She was in love.

When Sarah's best friend, Cindy, falls for a gorgeous guy, everyone's happy for her. The fact that he's an African prince is even better. But then Cindy starts acting weird, and Sarah and Tasha get worried. Is Ibrahima everything he seems to be? Join the gang for a slice of pizza and find out at 18 Pine St.